Hit List

Wait. She turned back, staring down at the fax machine. Something had caught her eye. A sheet of paper in the printout tray of the fax machine. Something was typed across it in 12-point Times New Roman, the default font for practically every application on every computer in the world:

HELP ME
37.4215, -122.0855
ALICE B

HiT LiSt

JACK HEATH

USBORNE

For my grandparents, Maisie and Bill.
I'm so lucky to be part of the family you made.

First published in the UK in 2012 by Usborne Publishing Ltd., Usborne House,
83–85 Saffron Hill, London EC1N 8RT, England. www.usborne.com

First published in 2010. Text copyright © Jack Heath, 2010

Aeroplane photo © Paul Chauncey / Alamy

The name Usborne and the devices ♆ ⊕ are Trade Marks of Usborne Publishing Ltd.

A CIP catalogue record for this book is available from the British Library.

ISBN 9781409531104

Prologue

Practice. It would take practice, but it could be done.

He moved around the empty room in circles, aerosol can in his hand, dodging invisible bystanders. Occasionally he paused, and stepped back with his head bowed, as if to allow someone to walk past.

The motions were easy. The more difficult part was maintaining an expression of faint surprise and curiosity – eyebrows up, head slightly tilted, lips curled into a lopsided grin. Like he'd spotted an old friend on the opposite side of a crowded room, and was going over to say hi. His intention was to look non-threatening, yet unapproachable to anyone who crossed his path.

He walked, he paused, he sidestepped, he kept walking. The only sound was the wind, keening at the broken window in the attic.

There were rumours that this house was haunted – rumours he reinforced at every opportunity. It would be inconvenient if someone purchased it and moved in. So he spent many nights turning battery-powered lights on and off in various rooms, throwing things at the walls to produce sudden thumps, and playing a battered violin in the attic. Whenever the estate agent brought prospective buyers around, they found fresh bloodstains on the floorboards, made from a foul-smelling syrup of red wine and barbecue sauce.

He didn't like to be disturbed. And he would disturb as many other people as it took to avoid it.

The walls of the room he was in were covered in mirrors. Every step of his complicated waltz was mimicked by the dozens of doppelgängers that surrounded him. He stared at them, trying to see himself as others would. They stared back, each with an equally suspicious gaze.

A twitch of his fingers, and the aerosol can vanished up his sleeve. A flick of the wrist, and it was back in his hand. He rehearsed this over and over, watching the can disappear and reappear as he walked. It's there. It's gone.

Now you see it, now you don't.

With his other hand, he loosened his collar, scratched his neck, ran his fingers through his hair. These motions would draw eyes away from the can, allowing it to come and go unobserved.

After a few more circuits, he came to a sudden halt in front of one of the mirrors. There was a picture taped to it – a teenage girl, on the footpath outside her school, unaware that she was being photographed.

He stared at her for a long time, memorizing every detail of her features. Then he closed his eyes and visualized them. Oak-brown hair, green irises, teeth not quite crooked enough to require braces. Narrow shoulders. Unpierced ears.

He opened his eyes again. Her hair was darker than he'd pictured, but otherwise, he'd been very close.

The girl was a chameleon, often hidden behind clever costumes and prosthetic make-up. If his plan was to succeed, if he was to have his revenge, he would need to recognize her instantly. He needed to know her face as well as he knew his own.

He reached out and touched the photo, tracing the curve of her cheekbones.

"Ashley," he whispered. Then he walked back to the other side of the room, and started weaving through the imaginary throng once again. Practice makes perfect.

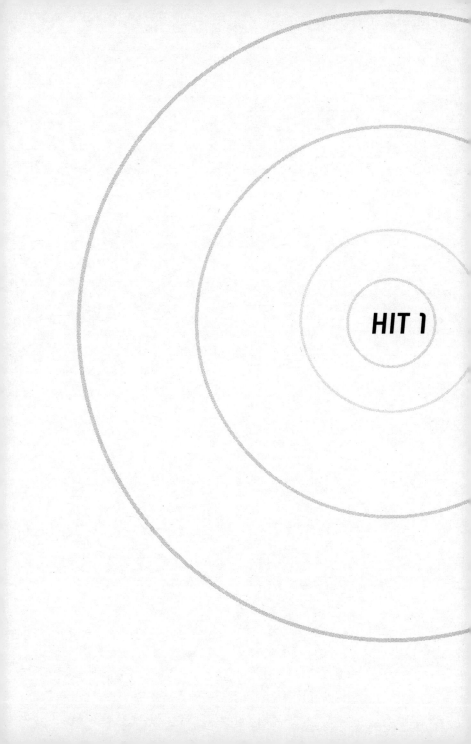

HIT 1

Mine Shaft

The guard stared down at the grubby pass card. "The thing is," he said, "you're not on the personnel list."

The girl blinked. Wiped the grime off her palms. "Sorry?"

"Your pass is valid," the guard said uncomfortably, "but I've got a list of people to let through, and you're not on it." Plus, he thought, I'm not sure I've ever seen you before.

The girl offered him a wry grin. "Does that mean I can go home?"

The guard sighed. "Well..."

"I know," the girl said, "you're not supposed to let me in

– it's against regulations. But if I leave, they're one worker short for the day and the foreman will say it's your fault. You could call him up here to sort it out, but then he'll blame you for wasting everyone's time." She scratched her hair under her cap. "'Course, if he'd done a proper headcount in the first place, there'd be no problem."

The guard wondered how long the girl had been working down in the mines. Couldn't have been more than a couple of years – she looked younger than his niece, although the tattoos on her neck made her at least eighteen. He looked at the pass card again. It was definitely legit.

"How about *I* call him?" the girl said, digging around in the pocket of her overalls. "That way—"

"No," the guard said. He jerked a thumb towards the mouth of the tunnel. "Go on."

The girl shrugged. "Sure. Have a good day."

The guard watched her walk away into the blackness. Then he stepped back into his booth, sat down in the swivel chair and picked up one of the wedding magazines his fiancée had left out for him. The interesting part of his day was over.

"Benjamin," Ash whispered, stripping off the overalls to expose a patchy grey suit, made from the same fabric as her cap. "I'm in the outer tunnel."

"What took you so long?" His voice was crisp and loud in Ash's ear, thanks to the new earphones they had bought. No more obvious wires on her neck – the plugs contained batteries that ran forty-eight hours between recharges, and were coated with rubber that matched Ash's skin tone exactly. Benjamin was on a boat half a kilometre offshore, but his voice was as clear as a freshly tuned piano.

"There was a list of miners," she replied. "But the guard was convinced by the pass card anyway."

"You're welcome."

Ash snorted. "Come on. It's not like it was hard for you to make, with your new laminating machine and Photoshop."

"Hey, you need more than just the equipment," Benjamin said. "You need the skill to use it. Did I say 'skill'? I meant 'genius'."

"Are you done?" Ash asked, distracted. She was walking as fast as she dared down the steep, uneven slope. Iron tracks had been bolted to the ground so mine carts could carry debris out of the shaft, and the wooden slats would have made good steps – but there was a sodium bulb bored into the roof every five metres, so Ash was sticking to the edge of the tunnel. Her camouflage was only effective in dim lighting, and she never knew when a mine cart might rattle up out of the gloom.

"Yeah, I'm done," Benjamin said. "If you need anything, you know where to find me."

"In my ear?"

"Like always."

The lights flickered momentarily as someone further down the tunnel started up a jackhammer, diverting a sizeable chunk of the electricity. Ash was glad of the din – now she would be inaudible as well as invisible.

The noise of the bit repeatedly striking the sandstone was like the clanging of a demented school bell. With a stab of guilt, she realized that school would be starting right about now. She hoped the forged doctor's certificate was fooling her teachers, and that the fake excursion note she'd given her dad had convinced him she was at the Museum of Art History. She'd installed an app on his phone, ensuring any calls he made to the school were redirected to a mobile with a fake answering machine message: *You've called Narahm School for Girls. All our operators are currently busy. Please leave your name, number and reason for phoning after the tone.* Any calls from the school to her father would be redirected to the same phone, but a different recording: *Hi, this is Ash. Leave a message for me or Mr. Arthur and we'll get back to you.*

But what if her father actually went to the school in person for some reason? What if the school sent a get-well-soon card to her house, and he saw it? What if—

Focus, Ash, she told herself. You've taken every possible precaution. You won't get busted. It's time to think about the job at hand.

The light was getting brighter and the noise louder. She'd almost reached the dig site. She could smell the broken rocks, and hear the whirring of the generator beneath the shouting of the miners. She kept her back to the wall, edging sideways down the tunnel.

The tracks had ended, and the grey dirt was getting finer beneath her feet. Time for the gross part. She spat into her hand, and wiped the saliva all over her face. Then she scooped up some of the dirt with her other hand and dabbed it against her cheeks, forehead and chin. The silty powder stuck to her skin and went crusty, like face paint at a carnival. She couldn't see herself to check, but hopefully she no longer looked like a disembodied head floating down the tunnel.

She'd reached the opening to the cavern. Slowly, silently, she peered around the bend.

Giant sodium lamps blazed in every corner, and six gas-analysis vents hummed on the walls – the modern-day equivalent of a caged canary. The miners shuffled around everywhere like ants in a nest. The woman with the jackhammer was near the centre of the cavern, the enormous machine shuddering in her grip. Ash had expected to see dust and smoke floating around the bit, but no – it was sinking into the stone as cleanly as a scalpel into butter, leaving holes the size of coins.

A metal walkway, about two metres above the ground, traversed the wall on the right-hand side of the cavern all the way from the tunnel she was in to the other side. There was a flight of stairs at each end.

It all matched the map, to which Benjamin had added everything the miners had constructed.

"I've reached the dig," she said. "How far away is the box?"

"According to your GPS and Mr. Buckland's map, it should be thirty-eight metres south-south-west of you, and about six metres down."

Damn it, she thought. "We've got a problem."

"Tunnel not where it's supposed to be?"

"Worse," Ash said. "The miners are digging in almost that exact spot."

"What?"

"Could they know about the box?"

She could picture Benjamin biting his lip. "No," he said finally. "They're a legitimate company. And they've been drilling here since before the map turned up. It's probably just coincidence. But either way, you—"

"Can't go digging for treasure while they're in there," Ash finished. "Right."

"So. Abort?"

"Hang on," Ash said. "Just a second."

She didn't want to give up, not now. She had assured the curator that she would get his artefact back, and she was so close!

Ash peeked around the corner again.

"There's another tunnel on the south side of the cavern," she said. "I think I can get to it. The miners won't see me if I stay close to the wall."

"Ash, that tunnel just goes deeper into the mine, all the way to the underground river. It doesn't curve back around or anything. You won't be able to come up at the box from underneath, if that's what you're thinking."

"It's not."

"Then what's the plan?"

Ash said, "You'll see."

She edged around the corner onto the walkway, feeling horribly conspicuous. But no one else was walking around the scaffolding – everyone was on the cave floor. She told herself that anyone looking up would have the wall-mounted sodium lamps in their eyes. With her camouflage, she would be little more than a shadow on the wall.

Her footsteps were soft on the metal grating – the mining boots looked heavy, but she'd hollowed out the soles and removed the steel caps for ease of movement. Of course, if a mine cart ran over her foot, she'd be—

"Hey!"

Ash's heart stopped. Run, or freeze?

She froze.

"Hey!" the miner yelled again. "Jennings!"

The woman with the jackhammer released the trigger. Looked up.

"Foreman wants to see you," the miner said. His voice echoed around the cavern.

The woman wiped some sweat off her forehead with a yellow glove, balancing the tool on its point with her other hand, and then passed the handle to the miner. He started drilling as she jogged over to the other side of the cavern.

Ash let the air out of her lungs. False alarm. She kept moving, one careful step at a time.

Two miners were rolling a cart along the tracks to the rocks broken up by the jackhammer, while another drove a Bobcat excavator towards them. The Bobcat's trowel descended, and the chunks of stone clattered against one another as they were scooped up. Hydraulics whirred as the Bobcat lifted the load, swung it sideways, and dumped it into the cart. A cloud of dust accompanied the crash, and the trowel swivelled back for another load.

The scaffolding Ash was on ended at a set of stairs, leading to the second tunnel. She slinked down, shoulder almost touching the wall. For a few frightening seconds, she was on the cavern floor with the workers – and then she was safe in the darkness of the tunnel.

"I made it," she whispered.

"To the other tunnel?"

"Yep." Ash removed her cap and tugged the elastic band off her ponytail with one hand, while removing a cigarette lighter from her overalls with the other.

"Great," Benjamin said. "And being in there will somehow allow you to sneak past the fifty or sixty miners?"

"Nope," Ash said. "But now I'll be out of the way when they leave."

She wrapped the elastic band around the lighter, tying down the button so a steady stream of butane flowed from the nozzle. Not enough to risk an explosion, not even enough to be detectable to the human nose – but just the same, enough to create a panic down here. She pitched the lighter back up onto the walkway.

A perfect throw – the lighter bounced twice on the grille before clattering to a stop right under one of the gas-analysis vents.

"Leave?" Benjamin was saying. "We can't wait for them to—"

An alarm shrieked, so loud that Ash had to press her palms against her ears. All work on the cave floor stopped instantly, and there was a moment of absolute stillness before someone yelled, "Gas! Evacuate! *Evacuate!*"

Tools thudded to the ground as the miners fled back towards the tunnel Ash had come in through. Their boots left dusty craters in the dirt. Someone hit a switch on the generator on their way out, and Ash watched it shudder to a stop.

She should have expected that. The miners wouldn't want to risk a short circuit while the generator was unsupervised – it was possible, though unlikely, for a spark to set the fuel tank alight.

The lights flickered and started to fade. Darkness grew from the corners of the cavern like squid ink.

In a matter of seconds, the dig site was deserted. The miners were well trained – at the first sign of toxic or explosive gas, stop what you're doing and get out.

Ash could hear Benjamin saying something, but she couldn't tell what. The alarm was deafening, and she had a growing suspicion that it couldn't be shut off.

"I don't know if you can hear me," she said, "but I'm okay. The alarm wasn't me. Well, it *was* me, but it's not *about* me. Don't freak out."

She raced up the stairs onto the walkway in the fading light, and snatched up the cigarette lighter. No sense leaving unnecessary traces. She pulled her hair back through the elastic loop and dropped the lighter into her pocket, then ran back down to the cavern floor.

The last of the lights had gone out now – Ash couldn't see a thing. Living in the city, Ash thought of darkness as her bedroom with the curtains closed, or a movie theatre between when the house lights go down and when the trailers start. But this was completely different. The blackness was so pure, so perfect, that when she waved a hand in front of her face, she felt the breeze on her cheek, but otherwise had no way of telling that she'd moved. In fact, for a surreal moment, Ash wondered if she'd simply *thought* about moving her hand, but hadn't actually done it, and the breeze had been something else.

The alarm was still blaring. They must be wired to an external power source. Anyone or anything could be in here and she wouldn't be able to see it or hear it—

Get a grip, Ash, she told herself. She fumbled for her phone, and snapped it open.

The glow of the screen was useless against the black ground – she had to crouch to see it, and even then it only illuminated the small circle in which she stood.

She selected *camera mode*, and pushed the button.

The flash lit up the cavern for a fragment of a second, like a mountainscape in a lightning storm. Ash regained her bearings – the jackhammer lay on its side at her two o'clock, the pile of spare hard hats and headlamps were at her eleven thirty. She jogged through the darkness towards them. When she guessed she was about three metres away, she took another picture.

The flash told her she'd underestimated; the pile of equipment was almost five metres away. She walked over and sorted through them until she found something that felt like a headlamp.

She clicked the switch. The bulb worked. She tightened the straps around her head, tilted the lamp so the light fell upon the ground roughly five metres in front of her, and ran back towards the jackhammer.

She had a collapsible trowel in her pocket, but now that she'd seen the kind of equipment the miners were using, she thought she could do better. She didn't know how to use the jackhammer, but there was a pile of shovels, mattocks and other digging tools nearby. Ash selected a pickaxe, swivelled it in her hands, and then swung it into the ground between her feet.

The rock crumbled easily – it was clearly a different substance from the stone the miners had been drilling through a few metres to Ash's right. Which made sense, she realized, since the box had only been buried here a couple of years. Not enough time for the mud to solidify into tough stone.

She swung again. The light jittered on the floor. She couldn't hear the rocks shattering over the screaming of the alarm, but she could feel the impact through the padded grip of the pickaxe.

Six metres down, Benjamin had said. But that was when she was up in the entrance tunnel, which was at least four metres above the cave floor. She should only need to dig down two metres. But the hole had to be fairly wide, or else there was a risk that she would completely miss the—

Clack. Ash paused. That last strike had felt different. Either she'd hit a tougher kind of rock, or she'd found what she was looking for.

She swept the broken stones aside with the blade of the pickaxe, and shone the headlamp into the hole she'd made.

Wood. She'd struck something made of hard wood.

She reached down and grabbed the box. It was scarcely bigger than an engagement-ring box, with dirty brass hinges and a scalloped handle. There was a scar on the top where the pickaxe had scraped it.

Reverently, she placed the box beside the hole. Lifted the lid.

Urgh, she thought. Success. She could have taken the object out so she could rebury the box, but she didn't want to touch it with her bare hands.

Shuddering, she closed the box again. "I have the prize,"

she told Benjamin. She tried to keep her voice from shaking. "Time to go."

Benjamin was talking, but Ash couldn't make out what he was saying. Probably asking her out, yet again, knowing she'd refuse. That was his usual way of congratulating her.

Ash started jogging back up towards the north tunnel. Now came the tough part: sneaking back out. The miners had all evacuated, so they would be watching from a distance as she emerged from the tunnel. Even if she put her overalls back on and wiped the grime off her face, they'd be curious, wondering why she'd taken so much longer than they had. She'd have to find a way to get past them without being spotted.

Or a place to hide, she thought, while I wait for them to come back in and resume work. But who knows how long that'll take? I have to be home by the time school finishes, or Dad will freak.

She kept moving. She couldn't strategize without seeing how far back the miners had evacuated. Maybe they'd be so far away that she could just walk out the mouth of the tunnel and head straight to the rendezvous.

A vague glow stained the tunnel wall up ahead – she was getting closer to daylight. She reached up and switched the headlamp off. There was no way of telling how long it would be before a hazard team got suited up and came down to search for the gas leak. If they rounded the corner further up the tunnel, Ash didn't want them glimpsing her torch.

She didn't think it was likely to happen soon, though. It seemed quiet and still up ahead.

Now that she was further away from the cavern, the alarm was growing fainter. "Benjamin," she said. "I'm coming out with the box."

There was no response.

"Benjamin?"

Nothing – except rustling of static.

Ash's heart kicked against her ribs. Had something happened to Benjamin? Had the local cops found him? If that had happened, she told herself, then there'd be no static, just silence. Right? It must be an equipment malfunction. Nothing to worry about.

The light was brighter now. She was almost at the guard station. Hopefully the guard would have evacuated too. He was suspicious of her before, he'd be even more suspicious now...

Ash rounded the last bend, and saw that the guard hadn't evacuated. He was slumped halfway through the window of his booth, broken glass stuck into his belly, a chunk of his throat torn out. There was a bullet hole in the wall behind him.

Ash's eyes widened. What the hell?

Then she looked down. And stumbled backwards, stifling a scream.

The miners were strewn all over the floor of the tunnel. Most had exit wounds in their backs. The rest had imploded heads. Ash could smell the blood, rank and coppery.

Someone had opened fire from outside the mouth of the tunnel. At first Ash imagined a psychopath with a machine gun, sweeping it from side to side with his finger on the trigger – and then she realized that the shooter's accuracy was too good for that. Almost every shot seemed to have hit someone in the head or the heart.

A sniper? No, too slow – a sniper wouldn't have been able to hit them all before they realized they were under attack and started running.

Then what the hell had happened here?

"Psst!"

Ash jumped. Jennings, the woman who'd been drilling, was crouched against the wall in the darkness. Her hand was covering a thigh wound – blood bubbled up between her fingers. Her face was white.

"Run!" she hissed at Ash.

And then her head snapped sideways, a half-second before the sound of the gunshot reached Ash's ears.

She clapped her hands over her mouth to stifle a scream. Her mind was whirling. A sniper couldn't do this, she realized.

But a dozen snipers could.

And even as Ash had this thought, she heard them. Boots thumping, ammo belts jingling. Sprinting towards the tunnel from outside.

Her paralysis broke and she ran, heart in her mouth, back down into the darkness towards the cavern.

As someone who existed outside the law – no, that was a cheap rationalization, she existed *against* the law – Ash was always living in the shadows of injury, prison and death. These things sometimes happened to normal people, but they were a lot more likely to happen to her. She was a criminal. A thief. She used to steal from good people to keep her family above the poverty line, now she stole from other thieves to atone – but it was still stealing.

Whenever she returned priceless artefacts to their owners, and saw their smiles and tears and gratitude, she had no regrets. But every time she was on a job and danger slinked out of the gloom, teeth bared, claws protracted, she wondered if the price was too high.

Part of her mind was reflecting on this now, as she sprinted down a pitch-black tunnel with a troop of snipers behind her and the stench of blood still in her nostrils. But most of her brainpower was consumed by other, more pressing questions: Have they seen me? Do they know I'm here? Who are they?

And most of all: How am I going to get out?

"Benjamin," she panted. "Can you hear me?"

Nothing but static. And suddenly she realized why – any group who could afford twelve snipers and a rifle for each would probably have radio-jamming equipment. She wouldn't be able to contact Benjamin until she was far away from the mine.

The cavern was just up ahead. She couldn't see it – the lights were still off, and the snipers behind might see her if she switched on her headlamp. But she could hear the echoes of her footsteps changing, getting quieter, going further before they bounced back. Sometimes at home Ash practised echolocation, moving around her house in the dark, clicking her fingers every few seconds, listening to the echoes to determine how far away the walls were. This was how bats saw the insides of their caves, how dolphins observed nearby predators, and how submarines detected incoming torpedoes.

When she felt the metal walkway under her feet, she turned left and clattered down the steps. She wanted to cut directly across the cavern floor to the south tunnel, instead of having to go the long way around along the scaffolding.

She could hear the snipers in the tunnel, but they didn't sound like they were running any more. Just walking quickly, and muttering to one another. They must not have seen me, Ash thought. Yet.

Sprinting across the blackness of the cavern floor was

nerve-racking. Ash couldn't help wondering if she'd misjudged her path, if she was about to trip over the pile of helmets or pitch head first into the pit where the box had been buried. But she didn't dare slow down. Any moment now the snipers might hear her, put on their night-vision goggles, and then a bullet would be erupting through her forehead.

BANG! Ash squealed, then clapped a hand over her mouth. That wasn't a gunshot. What could—

With a gargantuan crash, a stone block the size of a minivan slammed into the ground in front of her, spraying chips of rock that cut her face and palms. It had fallen from the ceiling of the cavern.

Cave-in! Ash whirled around and started to run back towards the north tunnel. She'd rather be shot than buried alive or crushed to pulp.

Then she heard the fizzing of climbing ropes, and looked up.

The cavern wasn't collapsing. Someone had blown a hole through the ceiling, and now they were abseiling down. She could see the beam of a headlamp swaying high above.

She couldn't go back to the north tunnel – she'd be shot. She couldn't keep running to the south tunnel – the fallen stone was in the way, and even if she went around it she'd never get there before the snipers or the abseilers arrived on the cavern floor. So she dashed into the space under the walkway, where she dropped to the ground and tried to look like a pile of rocks.

The first abseiler hit the ground as the snipers reached the walkway. He was shouting something. Ash couldn't hear the words, but she was a pretty good lip-reader: "Someone shut that goddamn alarm off!"

Seconds later, the klaxon choked mid-wail. The silence was so immediate that it took Ash's ears a moment to adjust.

"Thanks," the abseiler said. He was big – not tall, but broad-shouldered and thick-necked. There was something weird about his face, something alien. But it seemed less strange when Ash realized what it was: he had no eyebrows. They'd been shaved or burned off.

A second man landed beside him. Then a woman. They each unhooked the carabiners from their climbing harnesses, leaving them hanging a metre from the ground.

"What set it off?" the woman asked.

"Don't know, Sarge," the browless man said, drawing a pistol. "But I don't think it was us."

Three abseilers, Ash thought, plus five, no, six snipers. Nine against one. No fair.

"Hurry," the sergeant said. "The ghost's coming."

Ash tried to breathe as silently as possible. Had that woman said *ghost*?

The snipers clattered down the steps as the climbers

approached the hole. The browless man's handgun had a torch under the barrel. He pointed it in front of his feet as he walked. Now that he was closer, Ash could read the letters on the side of the gun: HK USP 45 CT.

Ash had never fired a gun, but she'd seen plenty of them. Too many. So she knew HK was the manufacturer, Heckler & Koch. USP stood for universal self-loading pistol, although she wasn't sure what the "universal" bit meant. The number 45 would be the diameter of the bullets, 0.45 inches, and CT stood for either counter-terrorist or compact tactical, she couldn't remember which.

These guys didn't act like a counter-terrorist unit. Ash didn't doubt that the government would be willing to slaughter fifty innocent people to get them out of the way – she had personal experience in that area. But why not just arrest the miners, steal from the dig site, then release them again with an apology? Terrorism Risk Assessment did that kind of thing all the time, and no one asked any questions.

So, not government. Heckler & Koch was a German company, but Ash couldn't detect accents in the abseilers' voices. No surprise – guns got transported all over the world, sometimes legally, sometimes not. Just because a pistol was manufactured in the Neckar Valley didn't mean the shooter had ever even been to Europe.

This group of murderers could be from anywhere,

working for anyone. And the letters on the side of the browless man's gun meant only that it could punch holes in Ash 0.45 inches wide.

"We're too late," the sergeant said. She was staring at the hole where Ash had dug up the box.

"I see that," the browless man replied. The other man said nothing.

"Could the miners have known?"

"No. But maybe they found it by accident."

The sergeant turned to the snipers. "Get back up to the entrance," she called. "Search the bodies. Get back down here when you're done."

They left wordlessly. No salutes, no "Sir, yes sir". They don't act military, Ash thought, despite the woman's rank. Ex-military, maybe? Private Military Corporation? The object in the box was worth millions of dollars – she could imagine someone hiring a corrupt PMC to retrieve it.

"Maybe the ghost got here before us?"

"Maybe," said the sergeant. "But I don't think so." She stared suspiciously into the darkness of the cavern. She seemed to look right at Ash.

There was no way out. Ash willed her body to stop trembling. If they saw her, she was dead.

"There's another tunnel," the browless man said. "Over there. We'll have to search it."

The sergeant said, "Harvey, you stay here, check this area. If you find anybody, kill them."

The silent man nodded. The browless man and the sergeant jogged towards the tunnel at the south end of the cavern and disappeared.

Ash had been worried that the deaths of the miners were her fault – she had driven them up to the surface, where they were exposed. But it looked like the soldiers or ex-soldiers or whatever they were would have killed them anyway. The only death she was responsible for was her own.

There wasn't much comfort in the realization.

Harvey turned away from Ash, and walked slowly towards the far side of the cavern.

Okay, she thought. Can't take the north tunnel – snipers between me and the exit. Can't take the south tunnel, because it's a dead end. And I can't stay here. Harvey will find me, or the others will when when they come back.

She had no weapons. She'd thought she would be dealing with harmless miners, not gun-toting sociopaths. She couldn't even rely on Benjamin – his boat was half a kilometre away, and there was no way to contact him without disabling the radio-jamming equipment. Which must be on the surface, probably near where they'd drilled the hole, because they hadn't brought it with—

The hole. Ash stared up at the bright circle cut into the

cavern's ceiling. Then her eyes traced down the climbing ropes to the carabiners hanging in a pool of light near the floor.

Could she climb one of them? All the way to the top, barehanded, quick, silent, without Harvey noticing and shooting her down?

There was only one way to find out. As a plan, it sure beat pretending to be a rock until the snipers came back.

Ash rose to her feet, hoping the camouflage dirt was still stuck to her face. As long as Harvey didn't point his torch directly at her, she would look like nothing more than softly shifting darkness.

She started to creep towards the carabiners, step by silent step.

She could see Harvey pacing parallel to the far wall, quickly and methodically. Methodical was good for her – predictable, easy to evade. Quick was bad; Ash wanted to be as far up that rope as possible by the time he worked his way in towards the centre. She changed her trajectory slightly to keep the block of stone that had fallen from the ceiling between him and her.

As she walked, she slowly unzipped her suit, wincing at the clinking of each tooth in the zip. She tucked the box inside its folds and zipped it back up so the wood was pressed against her belly. It wasn't too comfortable, but she'd need both hands free to climb the rope.

She was almost there now. The carabiner dangled a couple of metres in front of her. Ash had no harness, but it wouldn't have been very useful. Abseiling only works in one direction: down. Just the same, Ash clipped the carabiner onto her belt. At least if she fell, she would stop just above the ground – before Harvey saw her and shot her to bits.

Which is the worse way to die? she wondered. A broken neck or a bullet in the brain?

Now wasn't the time to think about it. She gripped the rope above her head, wrapped it around her hand twice, and pulled. The rope burned her knuckles, but held. She wound it around her other hand a little higher, and lifted herself up.

Only now did she realize how tough this was going to be.

Ash thought of herself as very fit. She cycled to school every day, and played no-rules soccer at lunchtimes. On Saturdays she'd jog to the pool, lifting rubber-coated three-kilogram hand weights as she ran, uncomfortably aware of how middle-aged they made her look. When she got to the pool, she'd swim a kilometre before jogging home. Exercise helped her think.

But now she was in a situation where her strong legs were useless. Worse than useless, because they weighed her down – muscle is eighteen per cent heavier than fat. Ash weighed almost sixty kilograms, which was much more than her hand weights. A lot to lift with just her arms.

She let go with one hand, reached higher, ignoring the burning of her triceps. Grabbed again, pulled again. You can do this, she told herself.

She'd learned that she could do amazing things when her life depended on it. The fastest she'd ever run was when a sociopathic hit man, Michael Peachey, had been aiming a gun at her back. Maybe, she thought, athletes would break more world records at the Olympics if they were being chased by tigers, or something. Someone should suggest it to the committee.

Grip, pull. Grip, pull. She was seven metres up now. Less than a third of the way.

The trick, she knew, was not to think about the aching muscles. Pain was not the same as injury – injury was physical, pain was mental. It could be controlled by focusing on other things. Like the gunman below. Like being silent so he didn't spot her.

She could feel the blood draining into her feet, making them swollen and heavy. She gritted her teeth, willing her legs to be lighter.

Ten metres up. Almost halfway. Five-elevenths, maybe. But it was only going to get harder from—

Click. Ash knew that sound. A safety catch.

She looked down.

Harvey was staring up at her, HK raised. His expression

revealed no surprise, as though it was completely normal to see a dirt-covered teenage girl in a camouflage suit climbing a rope with her bare hands in a mine that was supposed to be empty. Ash might have been offended if she weren't so terrified.

"Wait," she said.

Harvey's finger tightened on the trigger.

"You fire that, we both die," Ash said.

Harvey said nothing.

"You want to know what that alarm was for?" Ash said. "It was gas. The miners hit a vein of methane. Colourless, odourless, explosive. That's why they were evacuating."

Harvey said nothing.

"It's filled this whole cavern. The smallest spark could set it off. Why do you think they shut off the generator?"

Harvey said nothing.

"You pull that trigger, the propellant in the cartridge could ignite it. The explosion would vaporize us, and probably cause a cave-in."

Harvey said nothing.

Is he buying this? Ash wondered. I'm sure I look frightened enough for it to be true.

Harvey lowered the gun. Then he walked over to the mine cart, which was still filled with rocks. He picked one up. Hefted it.

Oh no, Ash thought. Get climbing! Now!

She started scrambling up the rope, faster than before, faster than she would have believed was possible. She heard Harvey grunt down below, and the rock whipped past her ear, so close she thought she felt the dust cascading off it. It sailed into the darkness and disappeared.

He'd missed. But Ash knew he had plenty more ammo.

She kept climbing. Fifteen metres up. Sixteen. Seventeen. Her arms felt like they were cooking from the inside out, like her bones were filled with molten lead.

A rock clipped her foot, and she gasped, nearly losing her grip on the rope. But she didn't. Nineteen metres – only three or four to go. She could see the sky through the hole above.

Come on, she told herself. You can do it!

Wham! A rock struck her square in the back, knocking the breath out of her lungs. Her fingers loosened, just a little, just an irresistible reflex, but it was enough. Before she knew it, she was falling, and when she tried to grab the rope again it whizzed through her palms so fast it burned her skin.

The ground rocketed up towards her. She raised her arms to protect her face, and then—

—with a *snap*, the rope tightened, digging her belt into her waist. The carabiner was attached to the front, so she was flipped over to face the ceiling so quickly it made her dizzy.

Her head and feet jerked backwards, like someone was trying to tie her hair to her ankles.

She grabbed the rope and tried to stand. As soon as her feet were on the ground she saw Harvey, standing by the mine cart. He grabbed two more rocks, and then kicked the cart away. It rattled down the tracks towards the south end of the cavern, so Ash couldn't get to it without first getting past Harvey.

Harvey held the rocks like he intended to clobber Ash with them rather than throw them. But he didn't move. His posture said, Surrender, or I'll hit you.

She didn't surrender. Wondering why he never talked, she bent and lifted the pickaxe she'd used to dig up the box.

Pickaxe versus rocks. Almost a fair fight. Except that his colleagues would be back soon. And Ash didn't know if her "Don't shoot or you'll explode" routine would work on them all.

"Get out of my way," she said, trying to sound as tough as possible.

Harvey looked at the pickaxe. Then he put down the rocks.

Ash expelled the breath she'd been holding.

Harvey picked up the jackhammer.

"The generator's off," Ash said. She heard her voice waver a little. "So that's pretty much just a really heavy knife."

Harvey pulled the trigger. The steel spike shuddered back and forth, ringing against both ends of its rail, the noise deafening. He smiled and tapped the side where it said *Hitachi Battery-Powered Breaker 33KG*.

Damn it, Ash thought.

She dived aside as Harvey lunged forward, the spike pointed at her heart. She swung the pickaxe at his head as he charged past, but he ducked under it, and a moment later they'd switched places and were facing each other again, circling like duelling swordsmen.

Jackhammers were designed to destroy things which had been made to be indestructible. Bricks, concrete, bitumen. Most of a jackhammer's strength came from its massive weight, so it worked best when pointed straight down. But even horizontally, Ash knew her muscles would be pulped and her bones would splinter if the spike touched her.

Harvey lifted the Hitachi and whirled around like a hammer-throw champion. Ash stumbled backwards as the spike swooped past, centimetres from her flesh, once, twice, before he stopped spinning.

How much juice has the battery got? Ash wondered. Without the generator recharging it, can I hold him off until it goes dry? But surely the snipers would be back by then – they must be able to hear the hammer.

She was outmatched in strength and firepower, but she

had advantages. She was maybe twenty kilograms lighter than Harvey, and the pickaxe was at least twenty-five kilos lighter than the jackhammer. That gave her forty-five kilos more speed and mobility than him.

So this time, *she* charged.

Harvey couldn't get the jackhammer's point up in time. When Ash drove the pickaxe towards his chest, he had to lift the Hitachi's handle to block it, leaving the spike pointed safely downwards. Ash's blade clanged against the steel so hard she felt the shock all the way up to her shoulder.

She didn't turn to face Harvey again – she couldn't win this battle. She kept running, headed for the stairs leading to the north tunnel.

She heard the jackhammer thunk to the ground as Harvey dropped it to give chase. He might be faster than her – if he was, the pickaxe wouldn't do much good. Not if he tackled her from behind. And even if he was slower, he could still trap her between him and the snipers. She had nowhere to go.

Or so Harvey would be thinking. Hopefully. But, Ash thought as her feet pounded the dirt, I've got something he doesn't.

She could sense him getting closer – she could hear his breaths, feel his thumping footsteps. By the time she'd reached the stairs, she figured he was four metres behind her at most.

She dashed up the steps three at a time. A second later she was at the mouth of the tunnel, with Harvey only halfway up the stairs. But she didn't go in. She could hear the snipers coming back down. Their shadows bounced against the tunnel wall.

Ash wrapped both hands around the rope attached to her belt, pulling it tight. She saw the dismay on Harvey's face as he realized he'd been tricked.

Because she couldn't resist, she shouted "Geronimo!" And then she jumped off the walkway and swung out to the centre of the cavern like Tarzan on a vine.

A cold wind blustered against her face as she pendulumed forwards. Her arms ached from the strain of lifting herself yet again, but she couldn't let the carabiner take her weight. That would leave her swinging too low – she'd slam straight into the stone block in the middle of the cavern.

Even now, as the block rushed up to meet her, she thought she might not be high enough. She pulled herself up the rope as she swooped towards the giant lump of rock, lifting her knees up to her chest. Come on, she thought. Come on, I'm so close!

Her butt actually grazed the stone as she flew over it. There was no time to feel relief. She hefted the pickaxe one-handed and started sawing through the rope with the underside of the blade. One slash, two, three—

Snap! She was free, and falling. She aimed her feet and, with a crash, landed squarely in the middle of the mine cart. Her momentum started it rattling down the tracks towards the south tunnel.

The limp rope swung back to the centre of the cavern, where Harvey was running desperately towards her. But Ash could tell he wasn't going to reach her in time. The cart was gaining speed as the slope increased, and soon the darkness of the tunnel had swallowed her up.

If Ash had remained in the cavern a few seconds longer, she would have seen the snipers arrive on the walkway, looking for the source of the commotion. She would have seen Harvey start to turn towards them – and then freeze, confusion in his eyes.

She would have recoiled as a blinding flash erupted around him, and covered her ears, too late to protect them from the horrible *crack*. When she looked again, she would have seen that Harvey had vanished into thin air, leaving only whispers of smoke and a rumpled set of clothes where he had stood a second before.

Ash would have heard one of the snipers scream, "The ghost! He's here!" before dropping his rifle and sprinting back up the tunnel towards the surface. She would have seen the others follow, panicked and desperate, like they were being chased by a pack of vicious wolves.

But Ash was already hundreds of metres away. She didn't see a thing.

Ash bounced painfully against the rocks in the bottom of the cart as it thundered through the blackness. The clattering of the wheels against the tracks rebounded against the walls until it sounded like she was surrounded by machine-gun fire.

She kept her head low. She had expected to feel sniper rounds hitting the cart from behind, but there was nothing. No gunshots, no sounds of pursuit. Weird, she thought. They must know there's no way out down here.

Which reminds me. How *am* I going to get out?

She could wait until they left, and think up something to tell her dad, and the school. Perhaps she could say she was spending the night at Benjamin's place. But she had the feeling that the soldiers wouldn't leave. Not until they found the box.

The question was, if she left it out for them to find, would they go? Or would they keep searching for her, until they—

Clang! Ash ducked down as sparks blossomed in the dark. She'd been wrong. The snipers were on her tail after all.

Hang on – that shot had hit the front of the cart, not the back.

Ash peeped over the rim just long enough to see the sergeant and the browless man in the tunnel up ahead, pistols levelled at the approaching cart. Another two bullets struck the front. Ash could see dents appearing in the metal on the inside.

It'll hold, she told herself. It's designed to carry tonnes of stone. Bullets only weigh, what, a couple of grams?

Then again, humans could carry many kilograms of stone, and bullets still hurt *them*.

She could hear the browless man shouting something. She couldn't tell what, but she could tell his voice was getting closer. The cart must be about to pass them.

Ash screamed as an arm plunged into the cart from above, swiping from side to side, the hand groping the air, searching for her. It missed, but caught the back rim as the cart swept past, and suddenly Ash had a passenger clinging to the rear.

The browless man's head appeared. His eyes locked onto Ash's as he gripped the rim with both hands and dragged himself halfway into the cart. He reached for Ash's throat.

She shrunk into the front of the cart, pressing her back against the wall. The man's fingers clenched in front of her face. She scrabbled at the rocks under her legs, grabbed one, and slammed it into his ear.

The man howled, and twisted sideways. Ash didn't try for a second strike. She just pushed her foot under his shoulder and kicked, as hard as she could. The man was shoved backwards out of the speeding cart. Ash didn't even hear him hit the ground.

The immediate crisis was over, but she was still in real trouble. As Benjamin had reminded her before they were cut off, this tunnel didn't go anywhere. So there was nothing stopping the soldiers from chasing the cart on foot, and catching up when the track ran out. As soon as the enemy knows where you are, be somewhere else.

She scanned the walls as they whipped past. Maybe there was a cave or a nook she could hide in...

Uh-oh. A barrier, up ahead. Clumsily scrawled spray-paint: *END OF TRACK*. Ash had thought she had more time. She reached for the brake – and then realized there wasn't one.

The cart was designed for rocks, not people. If there was a brake or a wheel lock, it would be on the outside where she couldn't get to it.

The barrier snapped in half as the cart plunged through it. Bits of wood whipped past over Ash's head. She searched for something she could use to stop the cart, but there was nothing in it except rocks. The walls of the tunnel were too far away to grab. She had a brief flashback to a science class – *every action has an equal and opposite reaction* – and considered throwing rocks forwards to decrease her momentum. But if one of them landed on the tracks, the cart could flip over, and she'd be crushed under the stones inside it.

With a *thud*, the cart reached the end of the rails, and kept going. It was just rolling along the dirt, Ash realized. It might flip over no matter what she did. And even if it didn't, the miners hadn't excavated much further than the end of the tracks. A wall was rushing up to meet her.

Ash didn't stop to think. A crash-landing was better than a straight-out crash, so she threw herself sideways out of the cart.

She heard it slam into the wall a split second before she hit the ground, shoulder first. She tried to roll with the impact, but it still felt like getting hit by a train. Pebbles and dust cascaded down the slope beside her, a slope she hadn't realized was there, and—

SPLASH! It was like being sprayed with liquid nitrogen. She screamed, her lips and nose stinging as the freezing bubbles squirmed out of them. She thrashed around until her head broke the surface.

The underground river. Of course.

The soldiers would never find her down here, as long as she stayed quiet. But a few minutes in the freezing black water would finish her off.

Something latched onto her foot. She wasn't alone.

She screamed again as a head rose from the water, something with big eyes and a deformed mouth that hissed and growled.

Ash swam for the riverbank, faster than she'd ever managed at the pool. But the thing was holding on to her too tightly. She kicked at it, trying to struggle free.

"It's me!" the thing whispered urgently. "Damn it, Ash, it's me!"

Ash looked back as the boy took off his scuba mask. "Benjamin?"

Benjamin grinned, his teeth bright in the suffocating darkness. "The one and only," he said.

"What are you doing here?" Ash demanded, her pulse still racing.

"When I couldn't get through to you, I checked the satellite feed," he said. "I saw some troops go in the front entrance, and some more break through the cavern roof, so I figured you'd take the south tunnel down to the river." He gave a smug shrug. "I know how your mind works."

Ash didn't tell him she'd forgotten about the river until she'd landed in it.

"So I took some scuba gear from the boat, swam along the cliff until I found the river outlet, then went upstream until I found you. You're not the only one with swimming prowess.

Or prow, in my case." He frowned for a second. "It's prow, right, not prowess? You know, because I'm male?"

"And now that you're here," Ash said, teeth chattering, "what are we supposed to do?"

Benjamin produced a second scuba mask. "Swim back out before we freeze to death. Hope you don't mind sharing an oxygen tank."

Ash could feel her fear unravelling, loosening its grip on her heart. She wasn't going to die — not today. "You're incredible, Benjamin," she said.

She caught a split-second blush before Benjamin's brazen charm returned. "Damn right I am," he said. "Let's get out of here."

Missing Persons

The daylight blinded her after the silent blackness of the tunnel. Ash squeezed her eyes shut as soon as she surfaced. The roaring of the waves was too loud, too close as they battered the cliffs.

"So who *were* those guys?" Benjamin asked.

Ash's teeth were chattering. Her fingers and toes were going numb. "There were nine of them," she said. "At least two males, at least one female. One man was named Harvey – not sure if that's his first name or last. They might have been ex-military, judging by their weapons and their skills, but not current, based on the way they talked."

"Not much to go on." Benjamin took Ash's glow stick and tucked it into the belt on his wetsuit. It looked like ordinary plastic in the sunshine.

"Doesn't matter," Ash said. "What counts is, they know even less about us."

"Anyone see you?"

"Harvey did," Ash admitted. "Heard my voice, too. And one of the others – a guy with no eyebrows. But I was wearing face camo, and they don't know my name. They don't know you or Buckland exist, either. We're in the clear, as long as we leave quickly."

Benjamin nodded. "The boat's that way. What about the miners? Did any of them spot you?"

Only one, Ash thought. Right before she got shot. "No," she said. An icy wave slapped her in the face, and she spat out some salt water before continuing. "The troops said something about a ghost."

Benjamin frowned. "Superstitious robbers?"

"Don't think so. It sounded like a real person, someone else coming after the prize. And they sounded scared when they talked about it."

"Just one more reason to hightail it out of here," Benjamin said, starting to swim towards the boat.

Ash sucked in one more lungful of air and followed him.

Maybe Hammond Buckland will know what they were talking about, she thought. I'll ask him when we give him his cut.

The boat was a fibreglass runabout with an inboard motor. Benjamin had left a rope ladder hanging over the side, and he held it steady while Ash climbed it.

"Did you find the box?" he asked.

"You didn't notice the unsightly bulge in my clothes?" she replied, clambering into the boat and reaching back down to grab his hand.

"Yeah, but I didn't want to say anything. Just in case."

"Just in case I was having a square baby?"

"Or you'd swallowed a Rubik's cube, yeah."

"Not today. It's the box."

He grinned as she pulled him up. "So we won. I like it when we win."

"It's a rare treat, for sure."

"Unless you count not dying as winning. We're pretty good at that."

"So far," Ash agreed.

"We should celebrate. Perhaps a romantic sunset picnic?"

"Perhaps not."

She unzipped her camouflage suit, pulled out the box and dumped it on a seat. There was a bag by the stern with some towels and a dry outfit in it – she peeled off her clothes and laid them out on the deck to dry before pulling out the towels and tossing one to Benjamin. He didn't catch it – he was staring at the box.

"Go on," she said, scrubbing her hair dry. "Open it. You know you want to."

"Is it gross?" he asked.

"Very."

Benjamin lifted the lid. He stared at the object inside, fascinated, and reached towards it – but pulled away without touching. He closed the box again.

"When you spoke to Harvey," he asked, "did you shout, 'This belongs in a museum!' like Indiana Jones?"

"Nope. Sorry."

Benjamin sighed. "What a wasted opportunity."

"There'll be others. I did shout 'Geronimo' at one point."

"Cool – were you jumping off something?"

"You bet. But I was wearing a safety rope."

"Still pretty awesome."

Ash had pulled on her jeans and was reaching for her T-shirt when she spotted something on the horizon. Now that her eyes had adjusted to the light, she could see another boat, floating in the distance. "Did the soldiers come by boat?"

"No," Benjamin said. "They were in white sedans." He followed her gaze. "Uh-oh. Cops?"

"I don't see any police markings." Ash lifted up one of the

seats, grabbed a pair of binoculars, and held them to her eyes. The boat was slightly larger than theirs, and appeared to be deserted. "No one on board," she said.

"Hope they dropped anchor. Otherwise it'll end up in the Pacific Trash Vortex." Benjamin had picked up his towel and started drying himself. "Did you know that most of the rubbish dumped in the sea by the USA and China gets dragged to the same spot by the currents? And so now there's an island of garbage covering over a million square kilometres?"

"No, I didn't know that," Ash said. Other than the mine, she thought, there's nothing along this coast for twenty kilometres in each direction. The miners arrived by bus. The soldiers arrived by car. So whose boat is that?

Hurry. The ghost's coming.

"Start the engine," she said. "We should go."

Two hours later Ash was in the Museum of Art History, right where she'd told her father to pick her up. She was standing outside the curator's office, now completely dry. While the swim had washed the grime off her, and the sunshine on the boat-ride back had thawed her out, she still felt terrible. Her shoulder was rapidly stiffening up, every muscle ached in both arms, and there was a ring of bruising around her waist where her belt had taken all her weight.

Benjamin had gone home. She didn't need his help to deliver the box, and they always made sure clients never saw them both together. They also used fake names, fake phone numbers, fake email addresses. That way, anyone trying to sell them out to the cops – or to the people they'd stolen from – wouldn't have enough information to go on.

The curator opened the door. He was a nervous-looking middle-aged man with curly hair and no wedding ring. He looked each way, as if preparing to cross a highway, before addressing Ash.

"Come in," he said.

Ash followed him into his office. He shut the door, and cleared a space on his desk.

"Is that it?" he asked, nodding to the box.

Ash put it on the desk, and opened the lid. The curator snatched up a pair of magnification goggles and studied the object inside.

Ash didn't know what he was looking for, exactly. But this artefact was over one hundred and twenty years old, and while it had spent most of that time in a police evidence locker in Arles, France, she knew it had spent three of the last four decades at this museum. It had been under the curator's care for most of his career – he'd had plenty of opportunities to examine it. If it was a forgery, he would know.

"It's smaller than I expected," she said, filling the silence.

The curator nodded. "That's partly its age, partly the way it was cut. And perspective, too – I mean, how often do you see one on its own?" He put down the magnifying glass. "It's genuine. Who stole it?"

Ash said, "That information wasn't part of the deal."

"Was it hard to recover?"

"You have no idea."

The curator looked like he had more questions, but was reluctant to ask them. He's smart, Ash thought. He realizes that the less he knows about what I've done, the safer he is.

He unlocked a cupboard, opened it, and took out a brick of cash. "Twenty thousand," he said, handing it to her.

Not a huge profit for Ash, Benjamin and Buckland. Not after the costs of flying out to the mine, hiring the boat, and purchasing the clothes and scuba gear, as well as the various expenses of the surveillance they'd been doing over the past few weeks.

But the money isn't why I'm doing this, Ash reminded herself. Not any more. Right?

She stuffed the cash into her school bag. "Pleasure doing business with you," she said. "I'll show myself out."

She opened the door and left, heading for the front entrance, leaving the curator alone with the mottled remains of Vincent van Gogh's left ear.

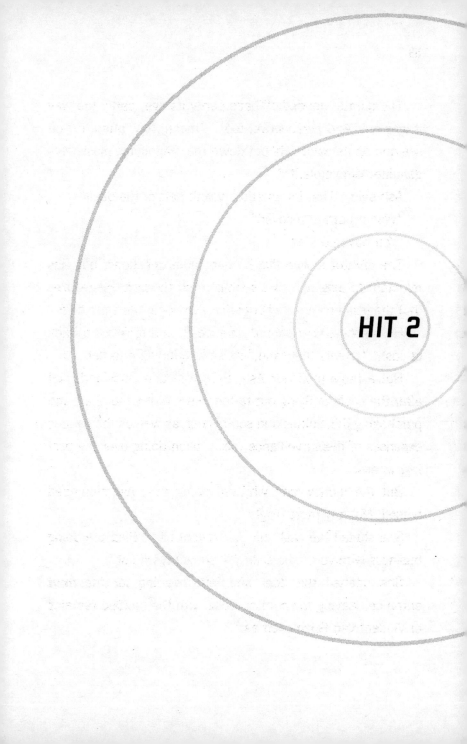

HIT 2

Appearances

"Hey, Dad," Ash said, climbing into the car and tightening her seat belt.

Her father flicked the indicator and glanced at the traffic in the rear-view mirror. "Yes?"

"Nothing," Ash said. "I just said hey. As in, hi."

"Oh, right. How was the Natural History Museum?"

"Art History, Dad. But yeah, it was intense."

Ash wasn't sure if her father had misspoken deliberately to see if she was paying attention, or if he was just preoccupied. Probably the latter – his constant state of distraction was the reason he hadn't noticed Ash's extra-curricular activities these past few years.

It was also how Ash's mother had been able to destroy him so thoroughly and unexpectedly. She left him when Ash was nine, and as a divorce lawyer, she was able to take half his money and most of his possessions. These days, he seemed to spend most of his time staring out the window at the garden, and though Ash never said so out loud, she suspected he was thinking about his ex-wife.

"Intense?" he said, finally getting the car moving. "They must've really jazzed it up since I was last there."

"Yeah, they have all kinds of stuff now," Ash said. "When was that?"

"When was what?"

"When you were last there." And if you've been there before, she thought, why did you think it was the *Natural* History Museum?

Her father squinted. "Not since you were born, probably. So what did you see today?"

"Some van Gogh," she said, suppressing a grimace. "A few cool things from Leonardo da Vinci's house in France. And a lot of stuff about cubism and cubists. Picasso, Braque, those guys."

If she had really toured the museum, she probably would have said, "Art stuff," and left it at that. But her father didn't seem suspicious of the extra information. Ash suddenly realized she didn't even feel guilty about lying to him any more – and then that *did* make her feel guilty.

"I got you a present," she said, as they pulled to a stop at a red light.

"Really?"

Ash passed him a coffee mug she'd bought at the gift shop on her way out. It had *The Scream* by Edvard Munch printed on it, with a subtitle under the howling man's face: *Two days without caffeine.*

He sighed. "Thanks, sweetie, but you didn't have to do that. You should be saving your money."

"It's a coffee mug, Dad. They're like, five bucks." Actually, the mug had cost her fifteen. But she had much more money than her father knew.

The light turned green, and they drove in silence for a while.

"How was your day?" she asked.

"It was okay," he said. "The clients told us they'd already designed the website they wanted, and then they emailed us something they'd knocked up in PowerPoint and told us to 'just write the code behind it'. So someone was going to have to go tell them, delicately, that they were all morons. I thought it was going to be me, but Bridget drew the short straw."

Ash tried to picture her father calling a boardroom full of

people morons. She couldn't – he was too polite. "Did you literally draw straws?" she asked.

"No. Random number generator."

She rolled her eyes. Of course.

Her father glanced at the clock in the dashboard. "Are you going to have time to change?" he asked. "Or should I take you straight there?"

Ash frowned. "Straight where?"

"The dance? At the school?"

Ash groaned. She'd forgotten about the school social. As far as the teachers know, she realized, I'm really sick. It'll seem very dodgy if I turn up tonight.

"I'm pretty tired," she said truthfully. "I think I'll give it a miss."

"Really?" Her father looked concerned. "But you'll miss the...dancing."

Ash shrugged. "We have dance class at school."

"What about the social-ness? The bonding?"

"I don't really need it."

Her father looked sceptical. "Name one friend you have besides Benjamin."

"Dad!"

"I never see you with anyone else," he said defensively. "And it's all very well to have a boyfriend—"

"He's not my boyfriend," Ash said. "I've told you that."

"—but it's important to have other friends too," her father continued. "And avoiding your classmates isn't going to help you make any."

"My classmates are boring!" Ash said. "They only care about clothes and bands and politics."

"Wouldn't hurt you to take an interest in that," her father said. "You'll be old enough to vote before too long."

"Not *real* politics," Ash said. "Clique politics. Gossip. Who stole whose best friend, that stuff."

"And what interests do you have that are so much more important?"

Money. Power. Adventure. "Computers?" she suggested.

Her father laughed. "Nice try." His voice softened. "All right. If you really don't want to go, I'll give the school a ring and tell them you're sick, or something."

"No!" Ash said. She could imagine how that conversation would go:

Hi, this is Ashley Arthur's father – Ash is feeling a little under the weather, so she's going to miss the dance tonight.

Sorry to hear that, Mr. Arthur. We hope her ear infection clears up soon.

What? I didn't say she had an ear infection.

It's right here on the doctor's certificate.

What doctor's certificate? What are you talking about?

Her father was staring at her. "I'll go," she said. "You're right. I might make some new friends."

"Uh, okay," her father replied, with a puzzled smile. "Good."

When they got home Ash went to her room and changed into a black halter top, grey skinny jeans, and a pair of ballet flats. The other girls would probably be wearing dresses, but this was the best she could do. The only dress she owned was the one she'd worn to an ambassador's house party, at which she'd stolen a 2,600-year-old transcript of *The Iliad*. She considered it too dangerous to wear the dress in public ever again, and planned to dump it in a charity bin in a couple of weeks.

My third costume today, she thought as she glanced at herself in the mirror. Not bad for someone who's not interested in clothes.

She walked into the bathroom and ran a brush through her hair, wincing as the bristles tugged at the knots. There was no time for make-up, but although she couldn't see it, she could still feel the mud from the mine on her face.

She dipped a towel in warm water and scrubbed at her face with it until her cheeks were pink. Then she rubbed in some moisturizer so her skin wouldn't dry out and become sore over the course of what promised to be a long, dull night.

"Dad," she called. "I'm ready."

* * *

"One, two, three, four, five," Ash recited into the breathalyser. It beeped, and the security guard withdrew it.

"Go on through," he said.

"Thanks," Ash replied. She retrieved her handbag from the other guard, who'd opened her water bottle and sniffed the liquid, but had otherwise left the contents untouched. Then she walked up the corridor towards the music pounding out of the gymnasium.

At a social two years ago some kids had smuggled in several bottles of booze, and after some visibly clumsy dancing one of them had vomited on the dance floor. In an attempt to keep the next year's social alcohol-free, the teachers warned the students that their bags would be searched on the way in.

Instead of not drinking, the students just did it before they arrived. There had been a long line of swaying, slurring, reeking teenagers outside the front entrance. Hence the breathalyser this year.

And Dad wonders why I don't hang out with my classmates, Ash thought.

Privately she hoped one of the kids would find another way to break the rules this year. Maybe then the school would cancel these socials altogether.

A dew of glitter coated the carpet outside the door to the

gym. Ash took a deep breath – the air smelled of hairspray and sweat – and crossed the threshold.

Lights whirled across the floor from an electric mirror ball up above. Ribbons were looped over the basketball hoops, curving down to the stack of speakers, where a dazed-looking DJ stood in front of the turntables with his finger resting on a button. The girls and boys stood on opposite sides of the dance floor, bobbing and shuffling self-consciously.

Only girls attended Ash's school – the boys were from the partner institution, Narahm School for Boys. Ash didn't know any of them by name, although she'd seen some of them before, hanging around near the school gates waiting for their girlfriends.

Ash wished Benjamin was here, but he didn't go to NSB. His mother had insisted that he study at a co-ed school, worried that his lack of social skills would be exacerbated by an all-male environment. Which, Ash admitted, it probably would have – if there had been anything wrong with his social skills to begin with.

Ash knew she should join a group and dance, blend in, but she was too tired even to pretend to have fun. She sat down on one of the plastic chairs that lined the gym wall, staring into space.

Despite what she'd told her father, she knew it wasn't just differing interests that separated her from her classmates. It was also the plethora of secrets that filled her life – secrets that could get her locked up, or killed.

She and Benjamin had only been working for Hammond Buckland for five months, but they'd been stealing things together for almost three years. And over time, Ash had become more and more detached from her acquaintances, since she hadn't been able to chat with them without worrying that they'd figure out her dangerous hobby. And what was the point of having friends she couldn't talk to?

Benjamin had always been her best friend. But now, she realized, he's my *only* friend. Is Dad right? Should I be trying to meet new people?

"Hey, Angie!"

Ash snapped back to reality. A girl was standing in front of her chair – curly black hair, earrings dangling almost to her shoulders.

"How are you?" the girl said. A greeting rather than a question.

"Hi," Ash said, not bothering to correct the wrong name. "Good, what about—"

The girl interrupted her: "I need you to check if Shane is looking at me," she said.

Ash peered past her at the group of boys. She had no idea which one was Shane.

"Yeah," she said. "Definitely."

The girl raised her eyebrows. "Oh my god. Wow. Thanks." And then she was gone.

Ash checked her watch. Two more hours of this.

Her eyelids were starting to droop. The chair was hard and stiff, but she was convinced she would fall asleep in it if she stayed there any longer – and that would draw attention.

She heaved herself up. The cafeteria would be open. Maybe a sugary, caffeinated beverage was the answer. She headed for the gymnasium door, eyes low and bleary.

She nearly collided with a boy who was walking in just as she was walking out. He jumped back when he saw her, startled.

"You okay?" Ash said.

"What? Yeah," he replied. "Sorry."

There was a pause.

"I didn't expect – you know," he said.

"What?" Ash asked, confused.

"You're just, uh," he said, "really pretty."

No one had ever said that to Ash before. She wasn't sure how to respond. Thank you, perhaps? But that sounded like agreement, which would seem immodest. So should she call him a liar instead? Surely that couldn't be the polite option.

The boy looked like he wanted to prolong the conversation, but couldn't think of anything to say. After a moment, he blushed and ran into the gymnasium.

Ash blinked. That was weird, she thought. I should find out who that was.

But not right now. It would be embarrassing to walk back into the gym, approach a girl, point to the boy and ask for his name – all while he was watching. And anyway, he looked a year or two older than her, so the girls in her year weren't likely to know him. Back to the original plan. Sugar and caffeine.

The cafeteria tables were crowded with fidgeting, nervous-looking kids, too shy to brave the dance floor. Most groups had both girls and boys in them. Funny, Ash thought, how they're happy to mingle *outside* the gym. I guess they're not as scared of each other as they are of the music, the lights, the dancing and what it's all supposed to mean.

She bought a can of an energy drink she'd never heard of, and sat down in a chair identical to the ones in the gym. She sipped, grimaced, and closed her eyes, listening to the conversation of the girls sitting on her left.

"...no, she only just messaged it to me."

"She was there? She videoed it?"

"No, someone else sent it to her. Everyone's messaging it to everyone. Everybody's got it."

"No one sent it to me."

"Yeah, well, I'm showing you now, aren't I?"

"Oh my god. Is that...oh my *god*!"

"I know, right?"

"Was anyone hurt?"

"It's night, doofus. Who's going to be in a library at night?"

"*You're* a doofus. Shut up. What about, like, security guards?"

Someone was moving towards the empty seat on Ash's right – a short ginger-haired boy who had dressed in a full-blown tuxedo. Ash avoided eye contact, took another sip from her can and willed him to go away. Don't sit here, she thought. This seat is reserved.

"Hey hey," the ginger boy said.

Ash looked at his face for the first time, and choked on her drink. "Benjamin?"

"Not if anyone asks," he said, grinning. "Officially I'm Jerome Tanner, footballer, percussionist, and student at Narahm School for Boys."

"What's with the tux?"

Benjamin stared at her, as though it was obvious. "It looks good."

Ash kept her voice low. "What will you do if the real Jerome shows up? You haven't...poisoned him or anything, have you?"

"Of course not." Benjamin plucked the can of drink from her hand and sipped it. "Urgh, gross. Of the one thousand

and sixty-six students at NSB, nine hundred and eighty-one have Facebook profiles. Of those profiles, six hundred and thirteen have lazy privacy settings that make them publicly visible. And of *those*, one had a status that read, 'Screw the social, can't be bothered'. Hello Jerome, and here I am."

He's clever, Ash thought, but he sure does know it. "You really don't look like a footballer."

Benjamin laughed. "If anyone says that, I'll just say, 'That's why I'm so good at it'."

"I'm not sure that makes sense."

"I'm not sure your face makes sense."

Ash stifled a giggle. "Don't get me wrong, I'm glad to see you, but why are you here?"

"I couldn't bear to be apart from you for another second," Benjamin said, sounding almost serious. "Also, I saw this."

He pulled a phone out of his pocket, tapped a few keys, and suddenly Ash was watching a video of a bald guy talking in front of the city library.

"What's this?" she asked.

"Just watch."

"Turn up the sound. I can't hear what he's saying."

"It's not important what he's saying," Benjamin said.

And then the library exploded.

Well, part of it. Ash recoiled as the side wall blasted outwards and an enormous ball of dust and smoke rolled out into the street. The man's eyes bugged out as he whirled around to face the noise. The camera wobbled, turned to the ground, then flitted back up to the library as the cameraman realized that this footage might be valuable. Even with the volume down so low, Ash could hear screams and the bleating of car horns. A refrigerator tumbled out the hole in the wall and thumped against the ground, spilling jars of mayonnaise and artichokes as it went.

"This footage was taken an hour ago," Benjamin said. "It's doing the rounds on the internet – when you next check your email, you'll find a dozen copies of the link in your inbox, probably with the subject line 'Terror attack at city library'. It's already today's most-viewed video on YouTube."

The footage was still going. Ash stared at the fallen fridge, stunned. "What actually happened?"

"The cops haven't released this yet," Benjamin said, "but according to my police scanner, an old water main burst in the staff kitchen. The circuit breakers got flooded and the building lost power for thirty minutes or so. The water drowned the pilot light in the central heating system, and short-circuited the photoresistor safety mechanism that's supposed to close the gas valve. So when the electricity came back on, the kitchen had filled with natural gas – which wouldn't have been a problem except that someone had left a stovetop burner on."

"Accidental?" Ash summarized.

"Definitely. There's no way anyone could have known that tonight was the night that pipe was going to pack it in. And even if they had, switching on the stove and putting out the pilot light is a pretty unreliable way of making an explosion. Plus, what's the motive? No one was in the building. They didn't even destroy that many books, since the explosion happened so far away from the—"

"So what does this have to do with us?"

"Nothing," Benjamin said. "Yet. I was just thinking about the hit list."

Ashley glanced around the room. No one appeared to be listening, or watching them.

Five months ago, when they had tried to rob Hammond Buckland, they'd failed. But instead of punishing them, Buckland gave them a list of one hundred stolen artefacts, complete with their current locations, their rightful owners, and how much each would pay to recover them. Homer's *The Iliad* and van Gogh's ear were just two of the six items they had already acquired.

"Wasn't there something in the city library vault that didn't belong there?" Benjamin was saying slyly. "Something that we have a perfect opportunity to liberate, now that the explosion has knocked out the alarms? Something that someone would pay sixty-five grand to get back?"

He gestured at the kids at the surrounding tables, gossiping and fiddling with their hair and playing with their phones. "Unless, of course, there's something else you'd rather be doing."

"Let's go," Ash said. She was going to have some fun tonight after all.

As she followed Benjamin out, she paused to throw her energy drink in the bin. As she turned back towards the door, she collided with the boy again – the one who'd complimented her and then fled.

Now that she got a better look at him, she found him quite attractive in a scruffy sort of way. He had kind eyes, and longish hair that seemed to know how much better it looked when messy, and had therefore resisted all his attempts to neaten it.

But she had work to do. She tried to step around him.

He rested a hand on her arm. "Wait a sec," he said. "I was thinking, that was kind of rude of me before. So maybe I could take you to a movie sometime? Like, to apologize."

"It's fine," Ash said, "you weren't rude. I've got to go."

He beamed. "In that case, maybe we could celebrate my non-rudeness by, say, going to a movie?"

Ash heard echoes of her own voice. *I'll go. You're right.*

I might make some new friends. Who would have thought that may turn out to be true?

She said, "You're really keen on that movie."

"I'm really keen on you," he said, and then immediately looked embarrassed. "Okay, *that* was rude. I'm sorry. Let me make it up to you by taking you to—"

She cut him off. "My name's Ashley Arthur – email me your number through the school network, okay? But right now I've really got to go."

He nodded. "Sure thing! I'm Liam, by the way."

"Nice to meet you, Liam," she said, meaning it. And then she ran out the door, where Benjamin was waiting for her.

"Who was that?" he asked, pointing.

Ash knew who he meant, but looked anyway. Liam was in the middle of some kind of victory dance, but stopped abruptly when he saw Ash staring. He jammed his hands into his pockets, trying to look casual, and failing.

"Uh, tell you on the way," Ash said.

The Vault

The city library was swarming with police. There were cops standing impassively beside the yellow crime-scene tape, cops shouting into phones on the library steps, and cops striding in and out the front door. An ambulance was parked on the grass just inside the tape, lights whirling atop it behind coloured plastic. Blue and red spotlights flitted across bystanders' faces.

It was all for appearances, Ash knew. They'd already classified the explosion as accidental. But because it was a very public disaster, the local government would want a very public investigation. When the voters picked up tomorrow's paper, they would see photos of numerous competent officers taking charge, doing everything that needed to be done.

Ash wondered how many people were being mugged and assaulted and killed elsewhere in the city while these officers were busy with their show of force. And then she remembered that she was a professional thief, and told herself not to be such a hypocrite.

"Wait – you said yes?" Benjamin sounded perplexed. "You're actually going on a date with this guy?"

They were in a car parked on the opposite side of the street from the library. They'd broken into it, but not to steal – it was just a convenient vantage point. Ash had checked the parking meter while she chained Benjamin's bicycle to it, and there were six hours left on the timer. The owner wasn't coming back any time soon.

"He seemed nice," Ash said, staring at the cops. A fake ID and some decent acting might have fooled that mine guard, but it wouldn't work on these guys. She was going to have to get past them without being spotted.

"What about me?" Benjamin was saying. "Don't *I* seem nice? What about the hundreds of times I've asked you out?"

"Thousands," Ash said. "But that's different."

"It sure is. I'm a guy who's been loyal to you for ten years. Whereas he's a total stranger."

"It's different because you do it as a joke," Ash said, becoming annoyed. "And he's not a stranger. I know his name, I know what school he goes to, and I know he thinks I'm pretty."

"Pretty?" exploded Benjamin. "You said yes to him because he called you pretty?"

"You've never said that the whole time we've been friends," Ash pointed out, surprised by how hurt he sounded.

"No, I haven't. I've said you were smart, I've said you were brave, I've said you were generous and reliable and one of a kind. But I guess none of that can compare to 'pretty', can it?"

"Will you just drop it?" Ash demanded. "We have work to do."

"Fine," Benjamin said, his voice bitter. "But for the record, I was never joking."

Ash looked away. They had been friends for way too long to attempt a romantic relationship – ten years, as Benjamin had just pointed out. Two-thirds of their lives. Couldn't he see that?

Had he really been pining after her since he first asked, when they were twelve? He'd never had a girlfriend, but Ash had just assumed it was for the same reason she'd never had

a boyfriend. They had been way too busy for dating.

"You're not going to be able to talk your way past those cops," Benjamin said finally.

"No," Ash said, relieved that he'd changed the subject. "I was just thinking that."

"So you'll need a way to get inside without them seeing you. Which means I need to provide a distraction."

Ash shook her head. "That's a twenty-metre gap between the tape and the building. It'll take at least five seconds to cross it, in which every single cop and reporter and bystander on that side of the library would have to be looking the other way. I don't think 'Hey, look over there!' will do the trick."

"I know. I've got something else in mind."

Two paramedics and an ambulance driver were leaning against the bonnet of the ambulance, eyes on the library, probably waiting for the police to tell them they could leave.

Benjamin watched Ash weave through the crowd towards them, trying to look as though her direction was random. She doesn't need to worry, he thought. Everyone out here is looking at the library. Everyone except me.

He scuffed the dirt with his cross trainers. *He thinks I'm pretty.*

How could she fall for that? Ash was the toughest,

cleverest person he'd ever met – but this Liam guy had turned her into such a...such a *girl*.

Benjamin knew he should let it go. He shouldn't have made her feel guilty. But how could she do this? Why would she choose some random boy over him?

Some random *good-looking* boy, said a voice in his head. With bright eyes and broad shoulders and big muscles and perfect teeth.

Benjamin scrunched his hands inside his pockets.

Ash was now standing as close to the ambulance as she could get without crossing the yellow tape. She's in position, Benjamin thought. He took a deep breath, and waited for the signal.

Ash looked across at him, and nodded.

Now!

Benjamin threw himself forwards, plunging through the throng of bystanders. Someone said, "What the hell?" as he ducked under the tape and sprinted towards the library.

He could feel the eyes of the crowd on his back. The yells and gasps became more and more distant until he couldn't hear them over his own furious panting.

The cops reacted quickly, running towards him only a half-second after he'd crossed the tape. "Stop right there," the nearest one roared. Benjamin only ran faster, heart thundering in his chest.

He almost made it to the steps before they got him. He felt a massive hand grab his shoulder, and another one close around his opposite forearm, and then he was being wrestled to the ground, one arm twisted behind his back.

"Stay down," one of the cops growled. Then, to the others, "I got him."

Don't screw this up, Benjamin told himself. Ash is counting on you.

"Let me go!" he screamed. "I have to find him! Let go of me!"

He felt handcuffs closing around his wrists. That was quick, he thought. I figured they'd just put me back behind the tape.

"Please, let me go!" he begged. "I have to help my grandpa!"

"This is a crime scene," another officer said. "What the hell are you trying to do?"

"He needs my help," Benjamin sobbed. "I need to find him!"

"Slow down, son. Who are you trying to find?"

He could hear the change in their voices – they weren't thinking of him as a teenage prankster any more. They thought they were dealing with a crazy person.

"My grandpa," he said. "I told you. Get off me!"

He was hauled to his feet. "Your grandpa's not here, kid,"

a policewoman with a pointed nose said. "Can we uncuff you, or are you going to make more trouble?"

"He's in the library," Benjamin wailed. "He phoned me, he's trapped, he needs help! Please!"

The police officers looked at one another. One of them said, "Get the paramedics." Then, to Benjamin, "Did your grandpa say where he was trapped?"

"Bottom level," Benjamin said. "The military history section. He said there was an earthquake or something, and a shelf fell on him."

The policewoman turned away and started talking into her radio. A stubbled cop with a thick neck said to Benjamin, "Come with me."

As Benjamin walked, he glanced over at the ambulance. Ash had vanished. He hoped he'd given her enough time.

It's up to you now, gorgeous, he thought. Good luck.

Ash watched the floor of the ambulance slide away, to be replaced by tyre-tracked grass. The legs of the gurney, emergency-yellow, unfolded in front of her until the wheels were resting on the ground. And then, with a clatter, she was on her way.

She felt horribly exposed, lying face down underneath the mattress, supported only by the frame of the gurney and the straps designed to restrain patients if they were seizing. She was pretty sure the two paramedics couldn't see her – her presence made only a slight lump in the mattress – but she was terrified of the police and the crowd of onlookers.

How would she appear to them? A dark shape, barely visible behind the frame and easily mistaken for part of the gurney? Or a completely visible teenage girl, strapped to the underside of it?

Turning her head, she couldn't see anyone else, just straps and bars. So they probably couldn't see her either. Probably.

Suddenly there was concrete under her rather than grass, and the gurney lurched and tilted so the blood flooded to her head and the straps bit a little tighter into her torso and thighs. She was going up the wheelchair ramp. If the paramedics were going to notice the gurney was forty-five kilos heavier than it should be – she'd removed the fifteen-kilogram defibrillator kit from under the frame to make room – it was going to happen now.

She clenched her fists by her sides. A while ago Benjamin had made a network of tubular balloons to go inside Ash's clothes, attached to a canister of compressed hydrogen sewn into her pocket. When she hit a switch on the canister, the balloons would inflate, halving her weight, doubling her jumping height, and increasing her running speed – as well as making her puff up like the Incredible Hulk. Unfortunately, hydrogen was extremely flammable, and the bulging clothes made her an easy target. They'd tried helium, but it was only half as effective.

Despite these drawbacks, Ash wished she was wearing the balloons now.

The journey up the ramp seemed to last an eternity. But the two paramedics didn't notice the extra weight. Each one probably assumed they were doing most of the work, while the other was slacking off. Ash felt the gurney level out as it reached the top of the ramp. The concrete changed to tiles, the noise of the crowd outside faded, and then she was in the library.

Good plan, Benjamin, she thought. I'm inside.

"This way," one of the paramedics said, and Ash felt the gurney change direction. The lifts must have been knocked out by the power failure. They were headed for another ramp.

The gurney lurched again – this time she was descending, feet first. The vault was on the bottom level.

"Do we know whereabouts on the bottom floor the guy is?" the paramedic asked.

"Yeah," the other one said. "Military history section."

The first one swore as the gurney reached the bottom of the ramp. "How the hell are we supposed to know where that is?"

"There's a sign. Right there."

The tiles changed to carpet. The gurney swerved, crashing through some double doors, and jolted to a stop. The wheels ceased clattering.

There was a second of silence. Ash held her breath.

"So where is he?"

"Damn it. Wrong section, or wrong floor?"

"I'll check this way, you check that way."

Footsteps receded away from the gurney to the left and right. Ash waited until they were very quiet, very distant.

"Mr. Fields?" one of the paramedics called. "Can you hear me?"

She triggered the release catches on the buckles holding her up – legs, then chest. She thumped to the ground, louder than she'd intended, and froze.

Silence.

"Hello?"

"Thought I heard something."

"Yeah, me too. Hello? Mr. Fields?"

Ash scanned her surroundings. Books, shelves, desks with built-in chairs. A couple of the bookcases had, she saw with surprise, fallen in the explosion. Benjamin's story about a trapped grandfather was more credible than she'd expected.

She couldn't see either of the paramedics, but she could

hear one of them approaching. She ran in the opposite direction, ducking between two bookcases and crouching behind a desk.

She saw one of the paramedics – a heavy-set man with frameless glasses – reappear near the gurney. "Can you hear me, Mr. Fields?"

Ash held still. The paramedic's eyes swept across the shelves and seats. She wasn't entirely concealed by the desk, but he didn't seem to see her. He was looking for an old man trapped beneath a bookshelf, not a teenage girl crouched under a desk.

He turned away, and jogged down another aisle. Ash let out a lungful of air, half-stood, turned around—

And saw the other paramedic approaching.

She dropped to the floor and scuttled away from the desk, heading for a dim triangular hollow beneath a bookcase that had toppled against the adjacent one. Then she realized that a fallen bookshelf was exactly what the paramedic would be searching for, but it was too late to change direction. She scampered into the darkness, palms flat against glossy covers, feet crushing open pages.

"Can you hear me, Mr. Fields?" the paramedic called. From his tone, Ash couldn't tell if he'd seen the movement or not.

She emerged out the other side of the tunnel, swerved left,

and ran down another aisle. The vault was just ahead – she could see a glint of steel between the rows of books.

Do I keep trying to dodge the paramedics until they go back upstairs? she wondered. Or do I try to crack the vault so I can hide in there?

She ran a quick risk-calculation in her head. The vault's door was carbon steel with a dual-control analogue combination lock, designed to be operated by two people, each knowing half the code. One hundred million possible combinations, 99,999,999 of which were rigged to sound the alarm. The walls were steel-reinforced concrete panels, thick and dense. The consistency of concrete is measured by its "slump" – how far it sags in the drying process. The greater the slump, the weaker the concrete. This stuff, Ash knew, had a slump of zero. It had been packed into the moulds rather than poured, and vibrated for hours to remove all air pockets. It was about as close to indestructible as human-made substances got.

But none of that would stop a thief who had the combination. And thanks to the button camera Benjamin had planted on the coat of one of the library employees weeks ago, Ash knew six out of the eight digits.

The vault, she decided. Seconds later, she was in front of the door, looking at the twin dials and the release button.

The flaw in dual-control analogue combination locks was that the person twisting the second dial could see the final position of the first, if they looked. This meant that they knew three quarters of the combination, not half. And thanks to Benjamin's camera, Ash knew it too.

She twisted the first dial clockwise to 1, and then anticlockwise to 61. Then she turned the second dial clockwise to 45, anticlockwise to 38, and hit the release button.

The door didn't open. Wrong combination. If the power had been on, an alarm would have started shrieking right about now.

Ash twisted the dials to 2, then 61, and 45, then 38, and pushed the button. Still nothing. She tried 3, 61, 45, 38.

This was why she and Benjamin hadn't attempted to break in before now – there had been a ninety-nine per cent chance she'd set off the alarm. But with the power down, all she had to do was be patient.

8, 61, 45, 38. The vault door stayed closed. 9, 61, 45, 38.

She could hear the paramedics clomping around elsewhere in the library. Hopefully they'd searched around here already, or at least wouldn't come this way until she was already inside the vault.

Ash tried 17. Then 18. Almost a fifth of the way through.

She wondered where Benjamin was. She'd advised him to run away from the cops as soon as they took their eyes off him, but she knew *he* knew that if he did, they would realize he'd been lying and call back the paramedics. Which would leave Ash in a tricky situation if she was still strapped to the underside of the gurney, waiting for an opportunity to escape.

She wasn't, but Benjamin had no way of knowing that – so he was probably still with the police, buying her as much time as he could.

The code didn't begin with 29. Nor 30, 31, or 32.

Get out of there, Benjamin, she thought. Don't get caught for my sake.

She tried 40, 61, 45, 38 – and heard a faint click inside the lock. She hit the release button, and heard a louder click as the wheel on the vault door spun a couple of degrees.

"Yes!" she whispered. She grabbed the wheel and twisted. After three complete rotations, the door clanked and swung outwards on well-oiled hinges.

And then Ash heard one of the paramedics approaching.

She slipped into the vault, grabbed the handle on the inside, and started to pull the door shut behind her. But when it was almost there, she froze.

He was too close. He would hear it when it closed.

Ash held the door a centimetre ajar and waited.

The paramedic's footsteps got louder. Ash held her breath as he walked into her field of vision, and stopped. He scanned the nearby bookshelves for signs of the phantom Mr. Fields.

Then he turned around and walked back.

Ash waited for ten long seconds, silently counting. Then she pulled the door the rest of the way shut. She clenched and unclenched her hands a few times, trying to stop them shaking.

The inside of the vault was as black as tar. The air was cold and dry – to better preserve the books, Ash guessed. She dug a penlight out of her pocket, clicked it on, and a circle of light appeared on the wall.

At first glance, the vault's contents were no different from the surroundings outside – just shelf after shelf of books. But as Ash drew closer, she could see that the books in here were significantly older than those in the military history section. Time had stained the pale covers and bleached the dark ones, leaving the titles difficult to read. Some had gold threads woven into patterns on the spines. Ash didn't touch any of them, worried that they would crumble to dust beneath her fingers.

Most of the books appeared to be laws, with titles that had words like *amendment* and *declaration* in them. A few novels were mixed in, too – she saw a first edition of *Bleak House*, and a handwritten draft of *Frankenstein*. There was a huge Bible that looked old enough to be the original.

What Ash was looking for would, she hoped, stand out among these ancient tomes: a four-terabyte portable hard drive, which held a program written by a Terrorism Risk Assessment employee, Kathy Connors, in her downtime. It would probably be about the size of two small laptops stacked one on top of the other, but Ash had no idea about the colour. She also wasn't sure exactly what the program did, but thanks to the size of the drive, she knew it must be something impressive. Four terabytes could contain about two thousand times the amount of code used to write Windows. And whatever it was, she knew it had got the programmer killed – her home had been burned down by an angry mob who were convinced she had murdered a child in a neighbouring suburb. The subsequent police investigation revealed that the child had never been anything more than a rumour.

How the drive had found its way from the blazing house to the city library vault, Ash had no idea. But thanks to the hit list, she knew it was here, and she knew the programmer's family would pay to get it back.

She was running out of places to look. She'd run her penlight over every shelf, and hadn't seen anything that looked remotely like a hard drive. She crouched down and started searching under the shelves.

Lights flickered on above her, and suddenly the inside of the vault was as bright as day. The cops must have got the power back up. Ten minutes earlier, Ash thought, and I would have set off the alarm.

A whirring sound, behind her.

Ash jumped. But it was only an old PC booting up. She hadn't seen it as she walked in – it was probably used to index the vault's contents, and rigged to switch on any time the door was unlocked.

Ash scanned the table the computer sat on, looking for signs of the hard drive. No luck. Just a phone, a fax machine, a modem and a printer. The set-up must have been decades old – these days, a single device would perform all the functions of those four machines. The computer chassis looked like it belonged in a museum rather than a library.

Ash stared at it. Where's the best place to hide a hard drive? she asked herself.

The answer was right in front of her. Inside a computer.

She kneeled beside the chassis and felt around the edges for a release catch. These old computers had lots of empty space inside them – even combined, the motherboard, processor, hard disk, memory card, video card and disk drives didn't take up much room, but the chassis needed to be spacious to keep the components from overheating. There might just be enough room inside for a clever thief to conceal a four-terabyte hard drive. It would be the perfect hiding place, since the computer chassis wasn't likely to be opened, and even if it was, the drive wouldn't look out of place to anyone other than a computer engineer. If she could just—

There! With a faint click, the wall of the chassis came loose, and Ash was staring into the innards of the computer.

Bingo. The hard drive looked much newer than the other components. Less dust, sleeker design. It was smaller than she had expected, but still conceivably large enough to hold 4TB of code. Ash unplugged it from the motherboard, put it on the floor, and reattached the wall of the chassis. Then she pocketed the drive, stood up, and turned to leave...

Wait. She turned back, staring down at the fax machine. Something had caught her eye. A sheet of paper in the printout tray of the fax machine. Something was typed across it in 12-point Times New Roman, the default font for practically every application on every computer in the world:

HELP ME
37.4215, -122.0855
ALICE B

"Have they found him yet?" Benjamin demanded.

"They're looking," the detective said calmly. "I've just got a few more questions for you while we wait, okay?"

Questions were bad news. Benjamin had been in the back of this police van for almost twenty minutes already, and the more questions he was asked, the more lies he had to tell. The more lies he had to tell, the more inconsistencies he had to worry about. Inconsistencies like –

"What exactly was your grandfather doing in the library at this time of night?"

"Reading, I'd imagine," Benjamin said. "That's what it's for, right?"

He regretted the words as soon as they left his mouth. Nobody likes a smart-arse, and Benjamin could tell by the detective's hardening gaze that he was no exception. He looked like a guy who'd been a cop a long time. Loose shirt, no tie. A mouth that had forgotten what a smile felt like. Eyes as dark and merciless as gun barrels.

"But it closed hours ago," he said. "Why was he *still* there?"

Benjamin looked at his feet. "Grandpa has Alzheimer's disease," he said. "He's pretty good, mostly, but sometimes he gets confused. You have to tell him things a couple of times before he hears them. I guess he just missed the announcement that they were closing."

The detective looked a bit sympathetic at that. Benjamin guessed that he, like most people, had an old relative whose mind wasn't what it once was.

"I'm sorry to hear that," the detective said.

"Thanks," Benjamin said.

His voice sounded familiar to Benjamin, but he couldn't work out why. A couple of cops had come to his school on career day, but they'd both been women, so that wasn't it.

I must have heard him interviewed on the radio, he thought, or something like that. It's not like I know any cops. Ash and I always try to avoid them, especially since—

His blood ran cold. What had this detective said his name was, again?

"Do you think maybe I could help with the search, Detective Smith?" Benjamin asked.

"Detective Wright," the cop corrected. "And don't worry, it's under control."

Detective Damien Wright. No way. This was the same guy who'd caught Ash five months ago at Hammond Buckland's headquarters. Benjamin had been listening as Wright interrogated her and handcuffed her to a piece of furniture – and as Ash escaped while he was out of the room.

Wright hadn't been able to track her down; she had given him a fake surname when he questioned her. But if he found out she was here, she and Benjamin were both in deep trouble.

But how can I warn her? he wondered. I can't use the radio while he's watching me. And if she's in the vault already, the signal won't get through the walls.

The detective must have seen the anxiety on Benjamin's

face. "All right," he said, standing up. "I'll go see if they've found any sign of your grandad."

"No!" Benjamin said. "I...uh..."

Think! he told himself. Come on!

"Don't just leave me here," he said. "On my own, I mean."

Wright sighed. "You can't come with me, kid. It's a crime scene." He stepped out of the van, leaving the door open. "Don't go anywhere," he said.

As soon as Wright was out of earshot, Benjamin grabbed his radio. "Ash, come in," he whispered. "Ash!"

There was no answer.

Ash picked up the sheet and reread the words.

Help me, 37.4215, -122.0855, Alice B.

What had she stumbled across? A prank? A test? A postmodern poem? Or a real-life distress call from someone who needed rescuing?

And then she no longer had time to think about it. There was a thumping on the vault door, and a voice, shouting, "Mr. Fields? Are you in there?"

Ash gasped. She'd assumed the paramedics had left. She ran behind a shelf, stuffing the paper into her pocket.

"Why would he be in there?" one of them asked.

"Don't know. But he's nowhere else in the library, so we have to check."

"I'll call the cops – maybe they'll be able to get the combination."

Scanning the area for a hiding place, Ash cursed Benjamin for his acting skills. If he hadn't been so convincing, the paramedics would have gone home by now, instead of standing outside an unlocked door, wondering about the combination. This would be funny, she thought, if it weren't so terrifying.

"Mr. Fields!"

"I don't think he's in there."

"If he's trapped, he might not be able to respond. He might not even be able to hear us through this goddamn—"

Clank. The door swung ajar, just a little. One of the paramedics must have touched the release button. Ash scuttled back towards it, ducking behind the carbon-steel frame. Hopefully the paramedics would be looking straight ahead at the shelves when they entered.

"What do you know – it's not even locked!"

The door was pulled all the way open, and the two paramedics ran in, one of them yelling, "Mr. Fields, can you hear me?"

Ash tiptoed sideways towards the door, quickly, quietly, willing them not to turn around. Almost there...

The paramedics were walking down an aisle, heads turning left and right. "I don't see him," one was saying.

Ash was almost there. She didn't take her eyes off the paramedics. Come on, she thought. Look harder. Search every aisle thoroughly.

She was three steps away. Two. One.

She was out! She turned to leave—

And crashed into a police officer. She yelped.

"Whoa," the officer said. "What are—"

Their gazes locked. Ash's eyes widened.

"You!" Detective Wright roared.

Ash heard the paramedics turn towards the noise. She reached back without looking, pushed the door closed, and spun one of the dials to lock it. Then she charged at Wright, who was reaching for the service revolver in his hip holster.

He was taller and heavier than her – she had no hope of knocking him down with this wild charge. So upon impact she wrapped her arms around him like he was an old friend, and squeezed as tight as she could, momentarily trapping his gun arm against his side as she reached for the radio on his hip.

Wright snarled, grabbed her hair with his free hand, and pulled. Ash squealed as her scalp burned and her neck twisted backwards. Her grip weakened, and she heard a snap as the stud keeping Wright's revolver in the holster came loose.

No, she thought. No!

He probably wouldn't shoot at her. But he wouldn't have to – at gunpoint, she would be forced to surrender.

She grabbed the revolver from underneath with one hand, forcing it up towards the ceiling. Then, even as he fought to bring it back down, she squeezed, pushing the cylinder out of alignment with the barrel.

Bullets jingled to the ground beneath her feet. Wright cursed, put his palm on her face, and shoved her backwards.

She stumbled but didn't fall. Bad move, detective, she thought. Now I'm out of reach – and you're unarmed.

She turned and sprinted for the double doors leading to the ramp. She could hear him giving chase, but he wasn't going to catch her. She was too fast.

When she got to the doors, she gave a nearby shelf a mighty tug before running through and pulling them shut. She heard books thudding to the floor and a deafening *WHAM* as the bookshelf fell in front of the doors, sealing them.

Ash didn't have time to rest. She had to get out of the library before Wright used his radio to warn the other cops about her.

She dashed up the ramp, slowing to a brisk walk when she got to the top. There was a uniformed cop near the information kiosk by the front entrance. He would see Ash any second now. Nothing she could do but bluff.

"Hey, Dad," Ash called. "Can we go home yet?"

The policeman turned to face her, a puzzled expression on his face.

"Oh, sorry," Ash said. "Thought you were my dad."

The cop said, "Who's your—"

"Wait, there he is," Ash said, looking through the glass door. And then she ran out, not giving the cop time to decide whether to stop her or not. She walked down the steps, crossed the yellow tape.

A radio exploded into life somewhere behind her. "All units be advised," Wright's voice said. "Homicide suspect in the area. Female, hair brown, height one-sixty, age approximately sixteen. Suspect is unarmed but dangerous."

But Ash had already disappeared into the crowd.

They barely made it back to school in time. As Benjamin squeezed the brakes and Ash let go of his shoulders – she'd been riding behind him, standing on the footrests they'd installed on either side of the rear wheel – she saw that the social was over and the other students were just starting to wander out into the car park. Some were laughing, a few were crying, and others were simply dazed by the abruptly halted music and raised lights which had suddenly turned the dance floor back into a school gymnasium.

She'd told Benjamin everything – the hard drive hidden inside the reference computer, the distress call in the fax machine, and her narrow escape from Detective Wright. Benjamin had filled her in on the detective's interrogation of him, and his subsequent escape from the van after Wright left him alone.

"He knows what we both look like, now," Ash said. "That's not good."

Benjamin shrugged. "I needed a haircut anyway," he said. "And besides, we both have alibis – people saw you here at the social, and as far as Mum knows, I'm still playing computer games in my room."

Ash saw her father's car pull in. "Got to go," she said.

"Wait – what are we going to do about the SOS?"

"Not sure," Ash said. "We should find out where the coordinates lead before we consider doing anything."

"They didn't look local. So wherever it is, we'd probably need Buckland's help to get there."

"Get there? Hang on – we're thieves, not a search and rescue team."

Benjamin frowned. "So what? We can't just do nothing."

"We can hand it in to the cops."

"And how exactly are we going to say we acquired it?"

He had a point. "We can drop it in anonymously," Ash said.

"Leading them to believe it's a hoax. What kind of hostage can get to a police station to deliver a distress call?"

"Maybe it *is* a hoax."

"And maybe it isn't. Anyway, what if where it was found is an important clue? The cops might not be able to help her without all the facts."

"You're suggesting that we keep them out of it and attempt a rescue mission ourselves?"

"We took the note," Benjamin said. "It's our responsibility now."

That's generous, Ash thought. *We* didn't take the note. I did.

Ash's father was climbing out of the car. "If my dad sees you here, we're both in trouble," she said. "Call Buckland. Tell him about the note, see what he says. Give him the drive, too. Okay?"

"Okay," Benjamin said. "See you later."

"See you," Ash said.

Traditionally, Benjamin punctuated his goodbyes by asking Ash out – for a coffee, to see a concert, to go skydiving. But this time he just started pedalling, gained some speed, and was gone.

"Ash!" It was her father. "Over here."

She jogged over to him.

"How was the social?" he asked.

"Surprising," she said. "Thanks for making me go."

Her father smiled. "Any time."

They drove home in comfortable silence. It wasn't until Ash was inside and walking past the kitchen that she realized she was starving. She hadn't had dinner before the social. In fact, she hadn't eaten anything since breakfast.

She microwaved some leftover pasta and wolfed it down. It wasn't great – her father rarely put much effort into his cooking when she wasn't around – but it filled the gaping hole in her stomach. Afterwards, she scooped some cold blueberry pie into two bowls and gave one to her dad. They ate in front of the TV.

Ash finished eating, washed the dishes, said goodnight and was shuffling towards her bedroom when her father called out.

"Ash?"

"Yeah?"

"Have you heard from your mother lately?"

Ash frowned. This was the first time he'd mentioned her in months. "No, why?"

"She hasn't cashed the last two cheques."

Ash's father was supposed to make regular alimony and child support payments to her mother, even though he was the one living with Ash and his ex-wife was the one with a well-paid job. How that was legal, Ash wasn't sure – she suspected it was mostly sexism on the part of the courts.

This situation occasionally eased Ash's guilty feelings about her criminal ventures. What was legal, she knew, wasn't always what was right.

"That's not like her," she told her father. "Maybe she's grown a conscience."

"Hey!" His stare was sharp. "That's your mother you're talking about."

I'm uncomfortably aware of that, Ash thought. "She ditched us. The fact that she's my mother makes that worse, not better."

He looked away.

"Anyway, I haven't spoken to her," Ash said. "In years."

Quietly, her father said, "Okay. Just asking."

Ash went into her bedroom and shut the door.

She never had trouble sleeping. She supposed that was the reward for leading an active life. Exhaustion. Her arms and legs felt heavy as she changed into her pyjamas, lifted the duvet, and tumbled into bed. Her eyes were closed before her head hit the pillow.

She was just starting to dream about Detective Wright – how his real first name was Alice, and the note was part of an elaborate trap to ensnare her, and now he knew her phone number because Benjamin had accidentally mentioned it and he was calling her, tracing the signal, storming towards her front door – when she realized her phone was actually ringing in real life.

She knocked a few things off her bedside table groping around for it. She blinked away the blur of sleep to check the caller ID. Benjamin.

"Benjamin," she mumbled, pressing the phone to her ear. "I'm sorry about before, I didn't mean to hurt your feelings or anything, it was just—"

"Forget it," Benjamin said. "Buckland wants to do this rescue tomorrow. And we'll have to be away overnight. Can you do it?"

"Wait," Ash said. "What? Away where?"

"Not sure yet," Benjamin said. "But Buckland said we'd be flying there, and that it'd take a while."

Ash yawned. "The school thinks I'm sick anyway – I can miss one more day. But why? What's going on? Does Buckland know who Alice is?"

"He said he'd explain everything on the way. Meet you at my place at eight a.m.?"

"Okay," Ash said. "See you then." The phone slipped out of her fingers as she tried to put it back on the table. She intended to pick it up, but the bed was so soft, and suddenly she was asleep again.

Beneath the Surface

"Peachey," the guard said. "You got a visitor."

Michael Peachey opened his eyes to see the same yellow concrete ceiling he'd been looking at for five months now. He'd stuck up some drawings of trees and bell towers – who would have thought prison would have an art programme? – but they only made the cell gloomier by contrast.

He'd been here for one hundred and fifty-three nights. He still had ten thousand, seven hundred and ninety-seven to go.

His anger had yet to fade. The government had paid him

to kill Hammond Buckland to save their failing economy. And now, the same government had locked him up for the murder – even though it turned out that Buckland wasn't dead. There was no part of this that made sense.

Peachey turned his head on the pillow to look at the two guards behind the thick shatterproof glass.

"Visiting hours are over," he said. "Get lost." He shut his eyes again.

"Visiting hours are when we say they are," the guard told him. He was a balding man, middle-aged, but had few wrinkles – he looked like the sort of man who didn't use his face enough to crease it. "Are you coming out, or am I going to have to come in and get you?"

Peachey remained still just long enough to worry the guard, then sat up. He swivelled on the mattress so his legs were over the side and then he dropped to the floor.

The prisoner in the bunk below awoke with a start. "Whoa, man, what are you doing?"

"Shut up," Peachey said, "or I'll tear your nose off your face."

The man fell silent. He was Peachey's third cellmate so far. The first one had attacked Peachey when he refused to vacate the top bunk, and Peachey had broken his jaw. The second had opened a letter from Peachey's lawyer; he was currently in a coma.

The new guy seemed smarter. He understood that Michael Peachey was a violent sociopath, easily provoked, and that the best way to survive a sentence at Hallett State Remand Centre was to stay out of his way.

Peachey pulled on his high-visibility orange overalls, turned his back to the guard, and put his hands through the slot in the cell door. The guard tightened manacles around his wrists, while a second guard watched. Peachey heard the slot at the bottom of the door open, and felt shackles close around his ankles.

"Step away from the door," the guard said.

Peachey did.

"Thomas, you going to be good?"

The other prisoner nodded.

The door was unlocked with a rusty crunch. The balding guard walked into the cell and looped a chain over Peachey's manacles and under his shackles, tightening it to keep his arms down by his sides.

"All right," the guard said. "Let's go."

He pushed Peachey through the door, followed him out, and locked it behind him. The other guard, a tall man with a thin moustache, prodded Peachey's back with a baton.

Peachey could feel the eyes of a hundred other prisoners, watching him from their cells. Gang members, bomb-makers, serial killers. Addicts who would gladly stab him for a single gram of meth. As the supposed murderer of a celebrity, he was used to being stared at – but it was harder to remain calm while he was in leg irons and his observers weren't.

The guards led him out of the cell block and into an exercise yard with featureless cement walls that were five metres high and almost as thick. There was a steel grille above, separating him from the starless sky. He suddenly wondered if he had a visitor at all. Maybe the guards intended to beat him to death with their batons, here and now. Maybe they were working for the federal agents who'd originally hired him. Or, perhaps, for Buckland himself.

Peachey figured he could knock down one of the guards with a headbutt, then jump onto his chest and stop his heart, or at least snap his sternum so he couldn't get back up. But he couldn't see a way to stop the other one from cracking his skull with the baton. If they were here to kill him, he was going to die.

He was led through the exercise yard, all the way to the door at the other end, without incident.

The visiting room was a dull, sterile hall, with two doors. One was marked *Visitors*, the other *Remandees.* There were eight small tables evenly spaced around the room, with four chairs bolted to the floor around each one. Three were brown, one was grey. The brown chairs were for visitors. The grey chairs were harder, with straighter backs.

When Peachey shuffled in, Detective Wright was sitting in a brown chair. He raised his paper coffee cup by way of greeting.

What the hell? Peachey thought. What's he doing here, at this time of night?

One of the guards pushed Peachey down into the chair opposite Wright. Wright sipped his coffee while Peachey stared at him.

Peachey was the first to speak. "You've found Buckland," he guessed.

"Not yet," Wright said. "But we will. Tell me where he is, and I'll get five years taken off your sentence."

"You don't have the authority to do that."

"Don't I? Maybe I know something you don't. Maybe some evidence was overlooked in your trial. Maybe enough to open it up to appeal, if someone were to bring it to the judge. But that won't happen, unless you help me find the body."

"There is no body. He's not dead."

Wright's face was inscrutable. "Serve the full thirty – see if I care."

Buckland can't stay underground for ever, Peachey thought. Someone will find him, sooner or later, and when it goes public, the government will have to let me out of here.

Wright wouldn't have come here just to offer Peachey deals he'd already rejected. Peachey said, "So what do you want?"

"I've found your accomplice," Wright said.

Peachey raised an eyebrow. "My accomplice?"

"Don't insult me. She kept my team distracted while you were hunting Buckland, and then she was with you when you killed him, standing nice and close so my sniper couldn't drop you. Plus, I saw you say something to her on your way out."

Peachey clenched his hands into fists behind his back. *Buckland's puppet*, he thought. *The one who knocked me out, and ran me over in a stolen car. Wright thinks she was working for me.*

"I don't know who you're talking about," he said.

"No?" Wright didn't look convinced. "Brunette, young, hell of a liar. Calls herself Ashley. Ring any bells?"

Ashley. Peachey smiled. *Now I know your name. When I get out of here, I'll get you. I'll make you lead me to Buckland, and then I'll kill you both.*

"Sorry," he said. "Don't think I know her. Did you get a last name?"

"Tell me where she is," Wright said, "and I'll get them to take off *ten* years. With good behaviour, you could be out of here by the time you're fifty."

"I thought you said you'd found her."

Wright flung his coffee into Peachey's face so fast he didn't have time to blink. He gasped as the fluid stung his skin – not hot, but ice-cold. Wright had been drinking a frappuccino.

"Last chance," Wright snarled. He was on his feet, reaching out, grabbing Peachey by the face and squeezing. "Where is the girl? Who is she? How do I find her?"

The coffee was trickling down Peachey's collar. He tried to bite Wright's hand, but couldn't – the palm covered his entire mouth.

Wright pushed Peachey against his chair, stepped back, and waited for a response.

"You're third," Peachey said, panting.

Wright said nothing.

"First Buckland," Peachey continued. "Then Ashley. And then you."

Wright didn't ask what he was talking about. "Before too long," he said, "you'll realize how many enemies you have among the prisoners, and how many friends *I* have among the guards. You'll wonder if you're even going to last thirty years." He shrugged into his coat. Buttoned it up. "And you'll wish you'd taken the deal."

He turned and walked out the visitors' exit. The door boomed closed behind him.

Peachey turned to look at the guards who'd brought him in, suddenly suspicious. Was Wright bluffing? Would he really try and have Peachey killed in prison?

The guards were gone.

He twisted his head left and right. The room was empty.

Peachey stood. Shuffled away from the chair, his movement restricted by the chains. He crouched for a moment and pulled his cuffed wrists under the shackles so his hands were in front of him, although he still couldn't raise them higher than his waist. Then he kept going towards the door. He didn't know why the guards were gone, but it might be an opportunity to escape. Wright may not have locked the doors on his way out, expecting them to auto-lock or thinking the guards would do it. And if the guards were gone...

"Hey! Hold it!"

Peachey stopped. He couldn't outrun anybody with these shackles biting into his ankles. He turned to see the guards had returned.

They were dragging two dead bodies.

Peachey stared. "What is this?"

The corpses belonged to other prison guards. One of them Peachey had met, though he didn't know her name. The other was unidentifiable – he'd been shot in the face, and he was missing his shirt, trousers and shoes. Both bodies bore numerous bullet wounds to the chest, dark circles ringed by singed fabric.

The two live guards arranged the bodies so they were sprawled just inside the door. The balding one pulled on some gloves, drew a pistol from a holster under the dead woman's arm, and advanced on Peachey.

Peachey staggered backwards, preparing for a fight. His heart was pounding. Headbutt, then jump, he thought. If I squat, I should be able to grab the gun – but can I hit the other guy with my hands trapped so low?

The guard turned away from Peachey, and fired two rounds into the wall beside the door. The shots reverberated around the room like the strikes of a timpani. The gun's slide locked back, revealing the hollow chamber.

The guard scattered a handful of shell casings across the floor, and then tossed the empty gun to Peachey. Peachey caught it.

"You're going to kill me," he said. "Pretend I was trying to escape."

"Wrong," the guard replied. He pulled a phone out of his pocket, and threw it over. "Keep this on you," he said. "But don't make any calls. Just wait for instructions."

"What kind of instructions?"

The guard turned back to the bodies. "The kind you're good at following."

Peachey's mind was racing. Who are these people? he wondered. Government? Military? Private? Why are they letting me go?

The guard pointed at the semi-naked body. "You'll find his

clothes out that door." He nodded towards the visitors' exit. "Wear them on your way out, for the cameras. There's a white Volvo parked two blocks east of here, registration YEF58K. It has a gun in the glove box, some clothes in the boot, and a fake driver's licence and passport with some cash and a credit card in the passenger-side seat pocket. The keys are in the front wheel-well on the driver's side."

"Who's the mark?" Peachey asked.

"I don't have that information."

"Who do you work for?"

"I don't have that information either." The guard took the keys from the dead woman's belt. "They won't know you're gone until rounds at six a.m. Between now and then, get as far away from here as you can."

He threw Peachey the keys. As Peachey was unlocking his cuffs, the two guards walked out the remandees' door and shut it behind them.

Within seconds, Peachey's wrists were free. He bent down to unlock his ankles.

Get as far away from here as you can. Sure, he thought. I've just got a few things to take care of first.

Three things, to be exact.

Ash woke up moments before her alarm. She grabbed the

purring phone, hit *cancel*, and sat up. Her brain automatically rewound through the previous night's events. The library. The detective. The distress call.

Buckland wants to do this rescue tomorrow. We'll have to be away overnight. Buckland said we'd be flying there, and that it'd take a while.

Where are we going? Ash wondered, uneasy. What does Buckland know that we don't?

But part of her was excited. Sometimes it felt like no matter how many things she returned to their owners, the guilt of her earlier crimes never seemed to sit any lighter. But this was something different. A *rescue*. She was going to save a human life. If that didn't ease her conscience, nothing would.

She went downstairs. Her father was already up, munching on some toast.

"You're up early," he said.

"I'm walking to school today," Ash replied. She took a bowl and some cereal out of the cupboard and put them next to the milk on the table.

"Alone?" her father asked.

"Only halfway," Ash said. "I'm meeting up with Alice at the supermarket."

The lie came easily.

"Have I met Alice?"

"I don't think so," Ash said. "But she's cool – I'll bring her over sometime."

She paused to spoon some cereal into her mouth.

"Actually," she said, crunching, "she invited me to her place after school today – she's having a sleepover party. But I told her I couldn't go."

Her father buttered some more toast. "Why's that?"

"Benjamin and I are going to see a movie."

Her father frowned, but said nothing. Ash picked up her bowl and spoon and took them over to the sink.

Finally, her father said, "I'm sure you and Benjamin could go to the movies some other time."

"Sorry?"

"I mean, the movie will still be there tomorrow," he continued. "Whereas the sleepover's only on tonight. And you and Benjamin are close – he won't take offence if you cancel, whereas Alice might think you're just not interested."

Ash pretended to think about it. "Well, maybe I will go to Alice's," she said. "Is that okay?"

"Sure."

Ash went back upstairs to get dressed, feeling cruel. It was one thing when we were poor, she thought. I *needed* to lie and steal back then. Now that we're back on our feet, can I justify this? Am I a bad person?

She thought of the museum curator, and the programmer's

family, and all the other people she'd helped. She thought of Alice B's message. *Help me.*

She and her father were doing fine, but other people weren't. She didn't want to retire while more people needed her. But there would always be someone. So could she deceive her dad for the rest of his life?

She put these thoughts out of her mind; she had work to do. She hefted her school bag and went back downstairs. Pushing open the front door, she called out, "See you after school tomorrow, Dad!"

From elsewhere in the house, her father said, "Bye, Ashley." And then she was out, headed for Benjamin's place.

The jog took almost half an hour. She would have liked to take her bike, but there was an outside chance her father would notice it was missing. Still, she liked jogging. The rhythms were hypnotic – the even breaths and footfalls, the thumping of her heart. Sometimes, when she was jogging for fun, she liked to try and synchronize them – two heartbeats for every step, a *ker* and a *thump*. Four steps per inhale, three per exhale.

Benjamin was waiting outside, punctual as ever. "Hey," he said.

"Hey," Ash replied.

There was a pause. Ash was feeling uncertain about the previous night's argument. Was he still angry about Liam? Or was he just depressed? Or was he over it, and she was worrying about nothing?

"Last night's kind of a blur," she said. "How are we getting to the airport again?"

"I've called a taxi to an address two blocks that way," he said, pointing. "Buckland's going to meet us at the terminal."

"Got it," Ash said. They started to walk.

After a while, she asked, "Did he tell you where we're going?"

"No."

"Or what we're doing once we get there?"

"No."

They'd already covered this. But for the first time since they'd met, Ash felt like she needed to fill the silence, to reach out across this horrible new distance to her best friend. She wanted to clasp his hand, but she was frightened he'd shake it off.

Benjamin asked, "Did the fax machine print out the message while you were there, or was it already in the tray?"

"In the tray," Ash said. "So it could have been there a long time, depending on when the vault was last opened."

"So we could be on our way to rescue a dead woman."

Ash nodded. "Unless Buckland has some way of knowing she's still alive."

"I don't see how he could. But it's not like he tells us everything."

"Sorry?"

Benjamin glanced back over his shoulder. "You know what I mean," he said. "Buckland's never explained where he got the hit list, or why he's still pretending to be dead, or where the X box is, as well as a lot of other things."

The X box was the last item on the hit list – the only one without a stated location or rightful owner. When they were first given the list, Benjamin asked Buckland what the X box was. Buckland said, very seriously, "You're not ready for the X box."

Then he had demanded to know why they were laughing.

"If he came out of hiding," Ash said, "the government would probably try to kill him again. Plus, Michael Peachey would be released from prison. And as for the hit list, it's not like either of us has ever asked where it came from."

"And why is that?"

"Because it doesn't matter."

"Because we're afraid of what he might say," Benjamin said. "What if he stole it?"

Ash chuckled. "Oh no! How horrid."

"I'm serious, Ash. What if he stole it from someone who might come after it? Or worse – what if he killed someone for it?"

She frowned. "He wouldn't do that."

"No? At least two people died at HBS when you were there. He doesn't seem too upset by that."

"They were murdered by government assassins, not Buckland."

"He arranged for the assassins to be there."

"One of the dead was a hit woman," Ash said, "who was about to shoot me."

"And who, if you recall, turned out to be working for Buckland."

"To protect him. It's not his fault she mistook me for someone else. And in fairness to her, I was trying to steal all his money at the time. If *you* recall."

Benjamin sighed. "Are you determined to be obtuse about this?"

"Obtuse? I—" Ash broke off, realizing that she was just bickering to stave off the silence. "I'm sorry," she said. "What are you trying to say?"

"Just that we should be careful. We can't just assume Buckland is infallible. Okay?"

"Okay." Ash smiled wryly. "You worry too much, but okay."

"I have to worry extra," he said. "You don't worry enough. We're here."

They stopped walking. Benjamin had chosen well – a big,

new house with a well-tended lawn and an expensive car in the driveway. A cab driver might find two kids headed for the airport on a school day curious, but coming from an expensive place like this, his or her curiosity probably wouldn't flare into suspicion.

"So," Ash said. "About last night."

"Last night," Benjamin agreed.

"When I agreed to go out with that guy, I didn't think about your feelings. That's not because they don't matter – it's just that I thought you were kidding, all those times you…anyway, I was insensitive. I'm sorry."

"It's okay," Benjamin said.

Ash sighed. "But I can't be your girlfriend," she said. "You understand that, right? We've been friends too long. I know all your flaws, and you know mine, and it just wouldn't work."

"It's okay," Benjamin said again. "I get it."

"You sure?"

"I'm sure."

Ash sighed, relieved. "Friends?" she asked.

"Always."

The taxi pulled up a minute later. The driver rolled down the window. Reading off a screen, she said, "Mr. Maitland and girlfriend, to the airport?"

Benjamin grinned. "That's us. Could you open the boot?"

The driver did. Benjamin took off his backpack and held out a hand for Ash's. "Let me take that for you, sweetie," he said.

Ash smiled warmly as she handed it over, and whispered through gritted teeth, "I'll get you for this."

"Worth it," Benjamin replied.

Every seat in the departure lounge was occupied by a prospective traveller. They grumbled sleepily, chewing spearmint gum, turning crinkled pages of magazines. The skin around their eyes was bruised with exhaustion.

Ash wondered why they all looked so tired, given that they were departing, not arriving. None of them could be jet-lagged – most of them wouldn't even have set foot on a plane yet today. Something about airports, she thought, just sucks the life force out of you.

Benjamin didn't seem to be affected. He was munching happily on an enormous cupcake with bluish-white icing he'd bought from the airport bar, which was called "The Termin-Ale". Ash thought the name suggested poison, and had said as much. Benjamin didn't seem to be put off.

"You kids lost your parents?"

Ash turned to see a chubby pilot, eyebrow raised.

"No," she said. "We're meeting them at the other end."

"Yeah," Benjamin said. "We're cool."

"What's your flight number?"

"AF5579, departing at ten forty-five," Benjamin lied smoothly. Ash guessed he was reading from the departure board over the pilot's shoulder. "You wouldn't be the one flying our plane, would you?"

The pilot frowned. "I would, actually. Why are you here so early?"

Uh-oh, Ash thought.

"Mum insisted," Benjamin said. "We told her that an airport was a pretty boring place to hang around for two hours – no offence, sir – but she wouldn't have it any other way."

"I see. Maybe I should get one of the flight attendants to find something for you to do."

Ash squinted. "Mr. Buckland? Is that you?"

Buckland winked. "Took you long enough."

"Wow," Benjamin said. Ash had to agree. Buckland was wearing something under his pilot's uniform so he looked fatter, and there was prosthetic make-up on his face, making his cheekbones seem lower and his chin broader. His skin was paler than Ash had ever seen it, and as she wondered if it was his natural shade, she realized that his proclivity for disguise had made her uncertain about what he really looked like.

"Nice costume," she said.

"Nice cover story," he replied. "If I didn't know you personally, I'd have believed every word."

"Can't say the same for you. Airport staff are never that helpful."

They followed Buckland out of the lounge, past the line of newsagents and bag shops and coffee kiosks until they came to a door marked *Staff Only*. They went through, and suddenly the polish of the airport was gone, replaced by concrete floors and greying brickwork. Exposed girders and power cables ran along the walls.

Buckland led them through a network of tunnels and into a hangar bay. It was so big that the back was cloaked in shadows, even though the gigantic doors at the front were wide open. There were a dozen planes inside, but the space shrunk them to the size of toys. It seemed to take a long time for them to cross to the far side, where Buckland's plane was.

It was a Bombardier Learjet 85, about twenty metres long, six high, and eighteen metres from wing tip to wing tip. Seven windows the size of tombstones sparkled along each side.

Ash had dreamed of someday owning her own plane – her mother's influence, perhaps, telling her that the greatest thing a human being could aspire to was affluence. But looking at Buckland's jet, she felt no craving, and little curiosity. I must be growing up, she thought. She supposed she should be happy about that, but it was hard to find satisfaction in a lack of desire. It was just that, a *lack*, the absence of something that had defined her for a very long time.

"After you," Benjamin said, and Ash realized that Buckland had already ascended the stairs. She followed.

The inside of the jet had only eight seats, two of which were occupied by boxes – Ash guessed that Buckland probably didn't have many passengers these days, since he was pretending to be dead. She walked to a seat facing the cockpit, and flopped down onto it. Benjamin took the seat next to her, across the aisle, and started fiddling with the controls on the side, presumably trying to extend the footrest.

"Still travelling in style, Mr. Buckland," he said.

Buckland shrugged.

Benjamin's chair suddenly swivelled to face the tail end of the plane, and then the seat tilted back until he was lying flat. "Whoops," he said.

"I'm afraid you'll need to fix that before take-off," Buckland told him. "And put your tray table up, et cetera."

"Ha ha."

Buckland opened the cockpit door. But before he could go through, Ash asked, "Where are we going?"

"California," Buckland said. He sat down in the pilot's seat, and flicked a switch above his head.

Ash and Benjamin looked at one another.

"California's a big place," Ash said. "Can you be more specific?"

"If Alice's coordinates were correct," Buckland said, "she's being held at the headquarters of the largest intelligence agency in the world."

"The CIA's headquarters aren't in California," Benjamin said. "They're in Virginia."

"Who's talking about the CIA?" Buckland touched a button, and Ash heard the engines come alive. "Strap yourselves in. We're going to the head office of Google®."

The Hunt

"I'm sorry," Henrietta said. "The seniors' library is closed today."

"Oh, okay," the bald man with the visitor's badge said. He smiled hopefully, his head still poking through the doorway. "Might I have a quick word with the librarian anyway?"

Henrietta sighed as she took the last few books out of the returns box. I'll lock the door next time, she thought. "Better make it *very* quick," she said. "I'll be out of here in a second."

"My name's Haley Price," the man said. "I'm from the National Arts Council. Some Year Nine and Ten students from this school exhibited their work at a function last week, and one of them left a piece behind. I was hoping to return it to her, and encourage her to submit something for the Craig-Martin Prize. She's really very good – and if she won, it could mean a grant for the school."

Thinking how tragic it was that an NAC representative apparently couldn't tell a library from an art class, Henrietta asked, "What's her name?"

Price put a large black folder on the desk and opened it, revealing dozens of paintings and sketches.

"Unfortunately, she didn't sign her full name on the piece. But it's a self-portrait, so I thought you might recognize her. She's clearly an intelligent girl, and in my experience, the school librarian tends to know the smart students. Ah, here we are."

He lifted out a sheet of faintly yellowed paper with a graphite sketch on it. In the bottom right-hand corner, there were some scribbled words – *Self-portrait, Ashley* – and a date. Despite Henrietta's annoyance at this interruption, she couldn't help but be impressed. The picture *was* good. The lines were hard and neat, the shading smooth and subtle. She was struck by the girl's expression – in most student self-portraits, the subject would be smiling, making eye contact with the viewer. Artists, she guessed, like everyone else, mostly saw themselves in mirrors and photos. But this girl was looking upwards, like she was searching for something. Her eyes held what looked like determination, and perhaps anxiety.

That girl really can do everything, Henrietta thought. No wonder Price is interested.

"That's Ashley Arthur," she said. "Definitely."

The man beamed. "You *do* know her! Terrific." He took a business card and a pen out of his pocket. "If I wrote down some contact details, would you be able to pass them on? Which year is she in?"

"Year Ten, I think. But you're better off going to the front office with messages."

The man nodded. "Of course. I..." He looked embarrassed for a moment. "Would you mind if I had a quick look at a yearbook? It's not that I don't trust you – but I'd get in a lot of trouble if I delivered the piece to the wrong person."

Henrietta nodded. "Sure."

She walked over to the yearbook shelves and ran a finger along the spines. Year Ten, she thought. Let's see – that would be...graduating class of...

BLAM!

Peachey lowered the gun as the librarian slumped to the floor, blood pouring from her ear. He stepped forwards quickly, bending down and pressing a handkerchief over the wound before the mess could reach the carpet.

Thinking of Buckland's resurrection, Peachey felt for a pulse. There was none.

He looked at his watch: 11.04. He'd been visiting schools near the old HBS head office for almost three hours now. Thank God he'd finally caught a break.

The blood flow slowed to a trickle as it coagulated. Peachey put his hands under the librarian's armpits and dragged her backwards, away from the glass door. One of her shoes came off. I'll get it later, he thought.

There was a supply cupboard adjacent to the library staff room. Locked. Peachey searched the librarian's pockets, but couldn't find a key.

Handbag, he thought. There'll be a handbag somewhere.

It was on the desk, near where he'd first seen her. Peachey rummaged through it, found the keys, opened the supply cupboard, and dragged the body inside. He went back for the shoe, and dropped it beside her.

There were half a dozen tubes of glue on a shelf next to the sheets of transparent plastic used to protect covers of library books. Peachey grabbed a tube on his way out. He also took the librarian's keys, and her cash, but not the wallet.

He closed the cupboard door, locked it, and squirted the whole tube of glue into the lock. Now no one was getting inside. Not without a locksmith, or maybe a battering ram. The corpse would stay hidden for days.

He went back to the yearbook section of the library, performed the same calculation the librarian had been halfway through to work out which book Ashley would be in, and then pulled it off the shelf. He flicked through to the mugshots, which were arranged alphabetically – hers was on the second page.

The librarian had been right. It was unmistakably the same girl he'd seen at HBS, right before he was arrested. Each picture had a caption with the usual nonsense below it. Hers read:

Name: Ashley Arthur.
Favourite subject: PE.
Favourite quote: "I have never let my schooling interfere with my education."
What I'll miss about NSG: The free wi-fi.

I see you, Peachey thought.

There was no more useful information, so he put the book back on the shelf and went back to the librarian's desk. He grabbed a pen and an A4 sheet of paper, and scribbled out a message: *The library is CLOSED TODAY. Sorry!* Looking for some tape to stick it to the door, he realized he'd probably sealed up every roll of it in the closet with the body. No matter. He pulled an anti-drug poster off the wall, peeled off the blobs of Blu-tack, and used them instead. Then he picked up his art folder and walked out, locking the door behind him.

Only one corridor separated the library from the front office. He walked slowly, pretending to examine the paintings on the walls as he went, although as far as he could tell, there was no one around to see him. Everybody was in class, students and teachers alike.

Some of the pictures were quite good, as good as what he'd done in prison. He felt a pang of regret. If he'd gone to a fancy school like this, he might be a famous artist by now.

When he got to the reception desk, the man who'd given him the visitor's badge said, "Find who you were looking for?"

"The sketch belongs to Ashley Arthur," Peachey said. "Would you be able to call her out of class so I could give it to her? Or should I wait until lunchtime?"

"Ashley isn't actually here today," the receptionist said. "If you give me the sketch, I can pass it on when she gets back."

Peachey shook his head. "Thanks, but I have to give it to her personally, or mail it via...come to think of it, do you have a postal address for Ashley?"

The receptionist sighed. "Not one I'm allowed to share. Perhaps you could come back on Monday?"

Peachey smiled. "I'll do that. Thanks for your help."

He handed over the badge and walked out. When he got to the car park, he held up the librarian's keys and pushed the unlock button. A blue hatchback chirped nearby, and he jogged over to it.

It felt good to have a new car. Whoever had gotten him out of the Hallett State Remand Centre had probably put a tracking device in the old one, and he didn't like them knowing his whereabouts while he didn't know theirs.

He climbed in, put on his seat belt and turned the key. It's a shame, he thought, that the receptionist was too well trained to give me Ashley's address.

But he wasn't worried. Now that he knew her full name, her age, and what school she went to, Peachey could find out everything else he needed.

"Google®? You're kidding."

Until Benjamin said it out loud, Ash had thought she'd misheard. Had Hammond Buckland lost his mind?

"Control Tower, this is Octopus 3," Buckland said, "requesting permission to take off." He twisted the headset mike away from his lips and turned to Ash and Benjamin. "Would I get dressed up like this and make you meet me at the airport just for a practical joke?"

Benjamin said, "But you do know that Google®'s not an intelligence agency, right?"

"Intelligence agencies are just organizations that collect information. And Google® has indexed more than two hundred and sixty terabytes of it. The CIA can't compete with that. Nor can any other agency."

"That's different. Government agencies collect *valuable* information. Secrets."

"Just because something's secret doesn't mean it's valuable," Buckland said. "And vice versa. Did you know that Google® can predict and assess outbreaks of disease quicker than any health organization, because of all the people typing in their symptoms?"

"I read about that," Benjamin admitted. "But that's just a quirk. It doesn't make them spies."

"There are a lot of other quirks like it," Buckland said. "Because the company has become so ubiquitous, it knows way more than most people realize. If you have a Gmail account, it knows your name and who you know. If you've used its maps, it knows where you live, where you study, where you work. If you have Google® Desktop, it knows everything that's on your computer. Most website owners use Google® Analytics, which tells them how many people are visiting their website, and for how long, and where they're from – so Google® knows all that too. Thanks to Google®

News, it knows what you're interested in. Did I mention that they own YouTube?"

"But none of that is useful information," Benjamin insisted.

"Individually, no. If Google® knows that Benjamin Whitely has googled plastic surgery, that's insignificant. But if fifty-two per cent of people in the state have googled plastic surgery, then that information *is* significant. And it can be checked for correlations – how many of those people have also googled protein supplements? How many of those are under twenty? And so on."

"Have you been monitoring my search history?"

Buckland frowned. "What do you mean?"

Benjamin reddened. "Nothing."

"We're missing the point," Ash said. "There is no way that Google® is kidnapping people."

"I didn't say they were." Buckland drummed his fingers on the plane's steering yoke. "I said Alice was being held at the Googleplex, their headquarters. My guess is, they don't even realize it."

"*My* guess is, it's a prank." Ash said. "Or a publicity stunt by Bing™."

"I'd agree with you," Buckland said, "except for the way it was done. As far as we can tell, only one message was sent. It was faxed – which is very traceable, by the way – to a locked vault in the city library. Publicity stunts have to be public. The same goes for pranks, since the prankster likes to see it happening. This is something else."

"But that's just as stupid a place to send a real SOS as a fake one," Ash said.

"Indeed. Which means she probably had no choice where the message ended up. Which means it's probably real."

"How the hell would you imprison someone at the Googleplex without Google® knowing about it?" Benjamin demanded. "Like you said, they know everything."

"We can figure that out later," Buckland said. "What we should be focusing on right now is how we can get her out." After a pause, he lifted the mike back to his mouth and said, "Copy that, control."

The pitch of the engine noise changed as Buckland's hands fluttered over the switches.

"So who is she?" Ash asked. "Any ideas?"

"How should I know?" Buckland replied. "There are millions of Alices around the world, and hundreds of thousands of Alice Bs. Plus, the fact that she didn't write her full name means that it's likely to be an alias."

"Or she was interrupted," Benjamin said.

Ash drummed her fingers on her thigh. "Are there any Alice Bs who work for Google®, or used to?"

"Yes," Buckland said. "I looked into that. There are four

that I could find, but I have no way of working out which it is – or if it is any of them. None of them has been reported missing."

I suppose we can ask her who she is after we rescue her, Ash thought.

Buckland turned away, his attention on the controls. The plane started to accelerate across the tarmac. The momentum pressed Ash backwards into her seat.

Benjamin turned to face her. "Are we really doing this?"

"Yeah," she said.

"Going to California, breaking into the Googleplex, rescuing a stranger?"

"Yeah."

He grinned. "Cool."

Ash's stomach lurched as the wheels lifted off the ground. The walls roared and vibrated, and Ash wondered if this was what the inside of a microwave sounded like. Out the window, the landscape gradually shrank until it was the size of a train set. Tiny cars trundled back and forth across ribbon-like highways, and a boat drew a white scar across the harbour.

The boat reminded Ash of the one she'd seen at the mine – and the fear she'd heard in the soldier's voices.

"Mr. Buckland," Ash said.

"Yes?"

"Have you heard of 'the ghost'?"

There was a long silence. Ash couldn't see his face.

He said, "Who gave you that name?"

It *is* a name, Ash thought. I knew it. "I overheard some other thieves talking about it," she said. "In the mine."

"Was he there?" Buckland sounded shocked.

With growing unease, Ash told him, "They said he was coming. And I think I saw his boat."

"Jesus," Buckland said. "You're lucky to be alive."

"Who is he?"

"No offence, but he's probably the most skilled thief in the world. In fact..." He paused.

They waited.

"You're freaking us out back here," Benjamin said.

"Do you believe in supernatural powers?" Buckland asked. "Psychics, seances, anything like that?"

Ash didn't hesitate. "Nope."

"No way," Benjamin agreed.

"Good," Buckland said. "The Ghost is a thief who likes people to *believe* he has paranormal abilities, both clients and victims alike. Everything he steals, he makes it look like magic, so no one knows how it was taken even after it's gone. One of his nastier habits is shooting people with a flash-bang, impaling them with a harpoon, and dragging them out of sight while the people nearby are still blinded, so the person appears to vanish. Sometimes he tosses a set of clothes onto the spot to confuse the witnesses further. It's supposed to make people scared of him, and it works.

"He has a website where clients post details about the items they want, and then try to outbid one another on them. He closes bidding on each item once he's stolen it, and then delivers it to whoever offered the most money. The last time I checked, the *Mona Lisa* was up to four hundred and fifty-four million euros."

"Like a criminal eBay?" Benjamin said.

"Yes – with only one seller."

"How does he know they'll be able to pay?" Ash asked. "Surely the internet is full of people who'll make bogus bids."

"Anyone who does that disappears," Buckland said. "Word got around, so it doesn't happen any more. A few people even got turned into zombies – you don't want to know how he does that."

"Actually," Benjamin said, "I kind of do."

"He injects them with a tiny amount of tetrodotoxin, which paralyses them, stops the breathing, lowers the body temperature, and slows the pulse down until it's undetectable, but leaves them completely conscious. Then he dumps them in a public place to be found and declared dead. There's no way of telling how many people he's done this to – some are cremated, alive; others regain their mobility days later, only to suffocate in their coffins or morgue drawers. But a few are able to escape, either by digging their way to the surface or screaming until someone hears, but they're too brain-damaged by the lack of oxygen to explain what happened to them, so all they can do is shuffle and moan—"

"Stop!" Benjamin said, slightly pale. "Okay, you're right. I didn't want to know that."

"How do you know so much about him?" Ash asked.

Buckland said, "I once owned the world's fourth-largest emerald, carved into the shape of the Buddha by Cambodian priests over a thousand years ago. When it appeared on the Ghost's site, I immediately took steps to protect it. I ordered a vault built out of sixty-six big steel bricks, stacked on top of one another and welded together. It cost me more than $130,000. There was no door – I figured I'd have the vault dismantled after I'd dealt with the Ghost some other way.

"Less than two hours after the emerald was sealed inside, he closed bidding on the site, claiming to have stolen it. I didn't believe it – how could he have got in? But when I went back to the vault, my guards had disappeared. I had security cameras, of course, so I watched the footage. And I saw the guards vanish in the blink of an eye, the Ghost walk towards the wall, walk *through* it, and walk back out, carrying the emerald."

"That's...impossible," Benjamin said.

"Indeed. I assume the footage must have been faked.

Someone could have broken into the security office, hacked into the computer and replaced the video file with a doctored one – difficult, but possible. I was rattled, so I went to the vault. It was intact on every side, but I still wasn't reassured. I used a cutting torch to cut one of the bricks loose. It took more than four hours. And when I finally got it out, I could see that the emerald was gone."

"How?" Ash was fascinated. "How did he do that?"

"If you ever figure that out," Buckland said, "I'll give you a million dollars to tell me."

"No evidence of blasting or cutting equipment in the vault?" Benjamin asked.

"It took another hour for the metal to cool down enough so I could climb in through the hole without getting burned, but when I did, the inside of the vault looked exactly the same as I'd left it. Except empty."

Ash said, "You're sure the emerald was in there when you sealed it?"

"I checked personally, before welding the final brick."

"It was the genuine article, not a hologram or something?"

"It was the real deal," Buckland said sadly.

"What about time loss?" Benjamin asked. "Are you sure it was only two hours between when you sealed the vault and when he put it on his website? You didn't black out, or anything?"

"No," Buckland said. "I was awake the whole time, and my watch stayed in sync with every other clock I've seen since then. It was only two hours – and remember, the vault took four hours to open later. The whole situation is impossible."

"Could the Ghost have built an entire fake vault?" Ash asked. "Stolen yours, left his behind, and extracted the emerald later?"

Buckland's eyes widened. "I hadn't considered that," he said. "But that would have taken dozens of people, heavy machinery, and probably a lot longer than two hours. Those bricks were a metre thick – the whole thing would have weighed several tonnes. And the Ghost wouldn't just have had to remove the vault and put a duplicate in its place. He would have had to rebuild the room it was in – no door was anywhere near wide or high enough to fit the entire vault through. That's very clever, but I can't believe it's the answer."

"It's a damn good trick," Benjamin murmured.

"It was," Buckland said. "And while I don't believe the Ghost can walk through walls, I do know he's very, very dangerous. Stay away from him. If you even hear his name, get as far away as you can, as quickly as you can."

Ash nodded. She wondered how close she had been to disappearing at the mine, and felt a little sick.

But that's the job, she told herself uneasily. Going into

dangerous places, doing dangerous things, meeting dangerous people. Putting yourself in harm's way, for the greater good, to make up for the bad things you've done. Right?

"Enough about him," Buckland said. "We've got a while before we land in California, and we should spend it talking about the Googleplex."

"How good's the security?" Ash asked.

"Extremely. Around-the-clock guards, cameras everywhere, every door locked electronically and only accessible using face-recognition software we won't be able to fool, or with a bypass code we won't have."

Benjamin said, "Do you know what kind of encryption algorithms the bypass uses?"

"Eight-bit, with a four-digit key," Buckland said. "But it doesn't matter, since the access panels are rigged to sound the alarm. Try to plug anything into the lock, and we'll be busted. Take too long punching in the numbers, and the system resets, which rules out using a calculator to work out a suitable combination by trial and error. So unless you can factor numbers bigger than one hundred million in your head, you won't be able—"

"I can," Benjamin said.

"—to crack the... What?"

"I can factor numbers bigger than one hundred million in my head," Benjamin said.

"No you can't," Ash said, frowning.

"Sure I can. I won a state mathematics competition for it last year. Give me one."

Buckland pulled a PDA out of his pocket and fiddled with it for a bit. "One hundred and fifty-seven million, two thousand five hundred and sixty-eight," he said.

"Two thousand, four hundred and eight," Benjamin replied. Then, as an afterthought, "And six thousand, five hundred and twenty-one."

Buckland fiddled some more, dividing his nine-digit number by one of Benjamin's four-digit numbers. "Say that again," he said.

Benjamin repeated the numbers. Buckland looked amazed.

"Benjamin," Ash said, "you have a superpower. Why didn't you ever tell me?"

"Well, I don't like to brag."

"You *love* to brag," she said.

Benjamin looked uncomfortable for a moment. "I've always been good with computers," he said, "I suck at sport and I read a lot. Having a freaky gift for maths would have made me a walking cliché of nerdiness, so I just never told anyone."

"Including me."

"I'm telling you now, aren't I?"

"Well," Buckland said, "that solves some of our problems,

but not all of them. All that stuff I mentioned is just Google®
security. Whoever has imprisoned Alice in the building almost
certainly has some kind of warning system of their own, and
there's no way to find out what it is. So you'll be improvising
a lot along the way."

My speciality, Ash thought. "No problem. What gear will
we have?"

Buckland nodded to one of the boxes on the seats behind
her. She unbuckled her seat belt and went over to it.

"I wasn't sure what we'd need," Buckland said. "So I
brought everything."

Ash opened the box. A power drill, glow sticks, a lock-
release gun, an EMP generator, and something that looked
like a grenade launcher from the future.

"What's this?" she asked.

Benjamin peered into the box. "Hey," he said. "That's
mine!"

"I know," Buckland said. "I took it from your lab. Thought
we might need it."

"Yeah, but…" Benjamin sighed. "Never mind."

"What?" Ash pressed.

"It was supposed to be a surprise," he said. "For your
birthday."

Ash stared at the thing, delighted. "Really?"

"Really."

"Thank you so much! I...what is it?"

"It started out as a grappling-hook launcher," Benjamin said. "Shoots the hook with one hundred and twenty kilos per square centimetre of pressure, so you can also use it to bust the hinges off doors – just make sure you unfold the stock like this and press it hard against your shoulder, otherwise the recoil could break your bones. Hold this button to rewind the cable, which is fifty metres long and can safely lift one hundred and seventy kilos.

"But I added this bit on the top – a tranquillizer gun with a twelve-dart magazine. It uses the same trigger as the grappling hook. Hit this switch to activate it.

"I also attached a bayonet, which you can extend or withdraw by pushing this button down here. If you pull the trigger while the blade is extended, it works as an electric saw." He scratched his head, clearly pleased with himself. "And here you've got a scope with night vision or thermal, a torch and a laser pointer. Best of all, because it's so narrow, it folds up and fits in a laptop bag."

"This is *amazing*," Ash said. "Where's the laser pointer?"

"Just behind this tinted shield. I got the diode out of a Blu-ray burner, and it's very powerful, so leave the shield on if you're just using it for targeting. Take it off if you want to set fire to something from a distance."

"Wow!" Ash wondered how long Benjamin had been

working on this. "It's by far the coolest thing I've ever seen. You know you could make a fortune selling this to the military, right?"

"I know," he said. "But yours are the only hands I'd trust it in. So I soldered a fingerprint scanner to the butt – once I install the reader software, only you will be able to fire it."

"What's it called?"

Benjamin frowned. "I hadn't really thought about it. Grappling-hook-tranquillizer-dart-saw-blade-gun doesn't exactly roll off the tongue, does it?"

Ash thought about the acronym – GHTDSBG. That was no good.

"It does an awful lot of things," Ash said. "We could call it 'the Benjamin'."

Benjamin flushed. "Thanks, but that would get too confusing."

Ash smiled. "How about 'the Benji'?"

He went even redder. "Whatever you want," he said.

Ash lifted the Benji up. It was surprisingly light – it would be heavier, she supposed, when it was loaded with the grappling hook and the darts, not to mention the batteries.

"Google® won't know what hit them," she said.

Invasion

"Escaped?" Detective Wright roared. "How?"

"We don't know yet, exactly," Belle said, her voice fuzzy through the speaker phone. "But it looks like he stole a gun from a guard, shot her and a colleague, took the keys and let himself out."

Her voice had taken on a flat, calm quality. Belle Evans had been Wright's partner for nine years, so he recognized the tone. It wasn't that she didn't care – she was compartmentalizing, becoming several people at once. One Belle was talking to him, and a hundred other Belles were looking at the problem from every angle, trying to work out where Peachey might have gone and how to get him back.

"How could they be so careless?" he demanded. "Michael Peachey is the most dangerous prisoner they have in that place. *Had*. He's a hit man – and a famous one at that."

"Former hit man. He probably lost his job when he got locked up."

"And for all we know he's got it back again now that he's out. Goddamn it." Wright grabbed his badge and his gun from out of the desk. He picked up the phone and switched off the speaker as he ran towards the lift. Maybe Peachey *is* back at work, he thought. Perhaps that's why he's out. If he had another job planned, he might have been waiting for the right time to escape – or perhaps it was me, somehow my presence helped him get out...

"There's a bright side," Belle said. "His fame should make him easier to catch."

"Maybe. Or maybe it'll just force him to become even more violent. We might have a dozen dead paparazzi on our hands by the end of the day."

"Hey, another bright side."

Wright's jaw already ached from clenching. "This is serious."

"I know." A few more Belles returned to the conversation. Tactful Belle and Sensitive Belle. "Sorry."

Wright pushed the button for the ground floor. The doors closed swiftly. "Get his picture out to every TV station and newspaper," he said. "Make it impossible for him to hide."

"That'll cause panic. There'll be citizen's arrests and beatings all over the state. He's too ordinary-looking – there must be hundreds of men in their thirties out there who look like him."

"Thousands. But if Peachey kills someone – which he will – and we didn't warn anyone that he was on the loose..."

"I know," Belle said. "I'm just saying we'll have to make sure every newspaper and TV or radio station that airs a warning includes a 'do not approach' quote from the force. That'll minimize the damage."

The doors opened. Wright stormed out into the empty foyer. "Good," he said. "Get a sketch artist to mock up a picture of him without his hair, and send that to the media as well."

"You think he's going to shave his head?"

"It's the first thing I'd do. And dig up our old sketch of Ashley and redistribute it. She's connected to this, somehow."

"Got it."

Wright hung up, and Peachey's voice echoed through his head, quiet, glacial. *You're third. First Buckland, then Ashley, and then you.*

Could I use this? Wright wondered. Could I follow him to Buckland's body, and then to Ashley, and have them both locked up by the end of the day?

"Excuse me," said a man in the doorway. "Detective?"

Wright didn't break step. "Whatever it is, talk to the sergeant," he said, pointing to a sign that said *All visitors please see reception*.

And then he looked.

The man was Peachey. He was smiling, and his head was shaved.

Wright reached for his gun, but Peachey was quicker. He lashed out, snapping Wright's nose like a dry branch.

I was right, Wright thought wildly, before blacking out.

Peachey would have liked to shoot Wright where he lay, but even with the silencer, his pistol would be loud enough to alert the sergeant around the corner, who would sound the alarm. And anyway, he was a man of his word – Wright would be killed after Buckland and Ashley Arthur, not before. So instead he dragged Wright over to a bench and propped him up in a sitting position, head slumped drunkenly.

The detective's nose had started bleeding. Peachey picked up a drinking-straw wrapper, crumpled it into a ball, and pushed it up the dripping nostril, half hoping Wright would inhale it and choke to death. There was a phone on the floor. Wright must have dropped it. Peachey put it in Wright's hand and placed his hand in his lap so it looked like he was sending a text message. No one would know he was unconscious unless they tried to talk to him.

Good enough. Peachey pulled Wright's wallet out of his breast pocket, checked that the badge was in it, and walked briskly around the corner to the reception desk.

"Can I help you?" the sergeant asked.

"Detective Mitch Pratley, North Central PD," Peachey said, holding up the badge and a Manila folder. "Here to drop off a witness statement for Damien Wright. He around?"

The sergeant wrote down the badge number, and then said, "Think you just missed him. I can—"

"No problem. I'll leave it on his desk."

Peachey pushed the button for the lift. The doors opened immediately, and he walked in, pushed the first floor button, and waited. Soon the lift was purring upwards.

He felt a curious thrill, infiltrating a police station. It was a first for him – he spent so much of his time avoiding cops that it was quite exhilarating being in the lion's den.

The doors opened. Peachey walked into the work area of the police station, surprised by how much it looked like an ordinary office – noticeboards, cubicles, blizzards of paper strewn across desks.

Only half a dozen cops were out on the floor, two typing furiously, three yelling into phones, and one striding along the corridor holding a USB stick in an evidence bag. Most of the force appeared to be out. Probably looking for me, Peachey thought with a smile.

There were four offices to his right. Two had closed doors, which Peachey guessed would be locked. One of the others was occupied by a hawk-nosed police chief who was typing a text message. The last office was open and seemed to be empty.

Peachey walked in, closed the door. Locked it.

The chair squawked as he sat down in front of the computer and switched it on. Immediately it asked for a password.

Peachey typed in *password*. An error message appeared: *Incorrect username and/or password*.

Peachey opened the drawers in the desk and started digging through the piles of paperwork. He found a photocopied application for a licence to carry a concealed weapon. It had the officer's birth date on it.

Peachey typed the date in. *Incorrect username and/or password*.

When the login screen reappeared, there was an additional message: *Final attempt before lockdown*. This meant that if Peachey got the password wrong this time, the computer would go into standby mode, and would refuse to switch on for an hour.

Peachey looked at the photos on the desk. There was one of a police academy graduation ceremony, and there was one of a man and a woman holding hands in front of the Leaning Tower of Pisa. Probably the officer and her husband or boyfriend.

There was an answering machine on the desk. Peachey hit *play*.

"No new messages and six old messages," the machine recited. "Message one."

"Hi, it's David," said a voice. "Just wondering if you'll be home in time for us to go to dinner at my mum's. Call me back. Love you."

Peachey typed *David*. The computer screen said, *Welcome*.

Peachey grinned. More than sixty per cent of passwords were the names of loved ones, birthdays, or the word "password", and there wasn't a hacker in the world who wasn't pleased about it.

He clicked an icon marked POACSD – the Police-Only Access Census Statistics Database. A menu popped up with search fields for name, age, gender, vehicle registration, address and blood type. Peachey typed in Ashley's name, the suburb her school was in, and her gender. He didn't bother typing an age range. He hit enter.

Only one match – age sixteen, address 146 East Park Way. There was a landline phone number, which Peachey wrote down on his hand. There was no mobile number or blood type, which was disappointing. No photo either, but he no longer needed one of those.

It seemed that Ashley had no criminal record, so all this information must have come from the census. Clever girl, Peachey thought. Never caught. But I'm cleverer.

He cocked his head to the side. A sound from the door – like someone turning the knob very slowly, very carefully, and finding it locked.

Peachey drew his pistol, checked the magazine, and slapped it back in. An unalerted cop would have knocked on the door or, if the office was theirs, used a key. Silently checking if a door was locked was SWAT behaviour. Somebody must have realized the station had been infiltrated.

The door might be kicked in and the room filled with tear gas in moments. Time to go, he thought. He picked up the computer monitor. Cords ripped out of the back with a series of dry pops. He carried it over to the window, and threw it.

The monitor shattered. The window didn't.

Peachey frowned. He'd been doing so well.

He tore down the blinds to see that the window had cracked, a spider's web of fissures scratched out across the glass. Peachey put his foot against it and pushed – the pane broke in two and tumbled out into the daylight. There were two SWAT officers standing in the street. One fired a shotgun in Peachey's direction while the other ran for cover behind the van.

The shot was too high. Peachey heard another window disintegrate above his head, the next floor up. He fired three rounds through the storm of falling glass, aiming for the running officer's back. The gun kicked in his hand, every shot like a thunderclap.

He'd missed – the guy was out of sight behind the van. Peachey turned on the guy with the shotgun and unleashed another eight rounds. Some missed, and some hit the Kevlar, but one punched through the SWAT officer's neck. He staggered backwards, firing again, too wide this time. Peachey had already stopped watching. The cop's lungs would be filling with blood. He was finished.

The door exploded behind him, and someone yelled, "Freeze!"

Peachey didn't. He vaulted over the window sill, plummeted, and hit the street with a hard thud. Then he was running, past the dying cop, past the van, and out into the unwary world.

* * *

"So how much money does Google® have?" a kid up the back asked loudly.

The tour guide maintained his easy-going smile. It was the kind of direct, impertinent question that kids often asked, not because they were interested, but just to make him uncomfortable. They didn't realize that he had heard all these questions hundreds of times before, and he'd had plenty of time to fine-tune his answers.

"The company's equity has been estimated at just over $36 billion," he said. "Enough to keep providing all our free services for many years to come."

At no point during his response had he stopped thinking about the pizza he intended to make for dinner. I need a new job, he thought. Something more challenging.

The sun shone down from a clear Californian sky on the Googleplex campus, painting the lawns an impossibly bright green, making the windows of the buildings gleam like gems. The teenage students seemed oblivious to the cheery surroundings – most of them, the guide thought, probably can't even see through their fringes.

Ding-ding! The tour group moved to the side of the path as a cyclist whirred by. When she neared Building 40 she dismounted, dropped her bike on the rack and jogged inside. Seconds later, someone else picked it up and pedalled away.

"Someone's stealing that bike!" a girl cried.

The guide shook his head. "The bicycles belong to the company. We leave them lying around the Googleplex so everyone can get from one side of the campus to the other with minimum fuss. It's fun, healthy, and good for the environment."

He saw the teachers nodding with approval. They liked it when he was a visibly good influence on the students. Maybe, he thought, it made them feel better about taking them on a field trip to a corporate headquarters, rather than teaching them English or science or something worthwhile.

This was a big group – he counted four teachers, which probably meant three classes. There were pros and cons of giving the tour to large groups of kids. It was easier to get them enthused, but harder to keep them focused, and he had to speak louder to reach them all. After two or three sessions like this one he always went home hoarse.

"Thirty per cent of our power comes from solar panels on the roof, where you'll also find endless pools—"

"Are they, like, the ones that go all the way to the edge of the roof?" a boy asked. A teacher shushed him while the guide answered.

"Those are called 'infinity pools'," he said, smiling. "Endless pools are like treadmills. Thanks to the artificial current, you can swim all day but never reach the far wall.

Unless you swim the wrong way, in which case you're likely to end up concussed."

The students giggled, as with every other time he'd made that thoroughly inoffensive joke. Olives, the guide thought. Feta, sun-dried tomatoes, smoked bacon.

They walked into the foyer of Building 41. The Google® employees barely glanced at them – tour groups visited almost every day.

"Before Google® came along, this campus was owned by Silicon Graphics, who—"

"I have to go to the bathroom," one of the girls said.

The teacher grabbed another girl and said, "Go with her."

Interrupt as much as you like, the guide thought. I'm paid by the hour.

He pointed at a door on the right as he spoke: "—who animated the dinosaurs in *Jurassic Park*, hence the *T. rex* skeleton you saw in the courtyard outside."

When the group reached the lift, a teacher ordered, "Sound off!"

"One," a student chirped.

"Two," another said.

"Three."

"Four."

The guide sighed. Presumably they would do this every time they went up or down a floor, to make sure they hadn't left anyone behind. It was going to be a long day.

The sound-off got to thirty-four and stopped. It seemed to the guide that there must be more than thirty-four kids, and sure enough, a teacher said, "Who's thirty-five?"

Silence.

A teacher produced a sheet of paper. "Karen Sloven," she read. "Karen, are you here?"

Silence again.

"Might she be one of the ladies who went to the bathroom?" the guide suggested.

"No," the teacher said. "They were Jemima and...who was the other one?"

Another teacher shrugged. "I thought she was one of yours."

They both looked at the other two teachers, each of whom shook their heads. They hadn't known the girl either.

"So we've got one student missing, and a girl *nobody* can identify in the bathroom?" the guide asked. He reached for his radio.

"Looks that way," a teacher said. He turned to the students. "Has anyone seen Karen Sloven?"

"Not since the bus," one of the kids said, eyes wide with excitement. The others were staring at the guide and the teachers with more interest than they'd shown so far. A missing student was an intriguing interruption.

The guide lifted the radio to his lips. He spoke quietly, so the students couldn't hear. "This is Tour One, calling security, Tour One calling security, over."

"Go ahead, Tour One. Over."

"Be advised, we have a student missing from the group, gone since arrival on the campus. There is also a potential intruder in the women's bathroom on the ground floor of Building 41. Both subjects are teenage, female, and wearing green school uniforms. Over."

"Copy that, Tour One. We'll send someone to check it out. Over."

The guide put the radio back on his belt. "Everyone remain calm," he said. "We're going to have to wait here until this is sorted out."

The students didn't look calm. They were whispering among themselves. Then talking. Then yelling.

Well, the guide thought, I wanted my job to be more challenging. "While we're waiting," he roared, "allow me to tell you about a typical day at Google®..."

Ash was just putting the lid back on the toilet cistern when there was a knock on the door.

"Hey," called the girl who'd been asked to escort her, and who seemed to resent her assignment. "Are you okay in there?"

"I'm fine," Ash said. "Sorry, I was just sending a text."

She didn't expect to find Alice this time – there were too many people around. This was just a reconnaissance mission, so she would be fully prepared when she came back tonight.

"They might leave without us," the girl said.

"They won't," Ash said. She put on her backpack, now empty, flushed the toilet for form's sake, and then opened the door. The girl was chewing a nail anxiously.

"Hurry up," she said as Ash washed her hands. "I need to know all about Google® for my assignment."

"I know more about Google® than the guide does." Ash prodded the soap dispenser. "Ask me anything."

"Okay: how long does it take Google® tour guides to forget that they're missing two people?"

"Longer than this," Ash said. "Relax."

"You sound weird. Where'd you say you were from?"

Ash had thought her fake West Coast USA accent was pretty good. Not good enough, apparently. "My parents moved here from Idaho," she said, picking a state at random.

They walked back out into the Building 41 foyer, where they'd last seen the tour group. They were gone.

"Fantastic," the girl said. "You were saying?"

There was a sign on the wall: *Elevators C*. "They'll be that way," Ash said.

"How do you know that?"

"Because otherwise the guide could only show us the ground floor."

There were two security guards approaching. They hadn't spotted the two girls yet.

Uh-oh, Ash thought. I thought I'd have more time.

"Let's ask them," the girl said, pointing.

"Good idea," Ash said. But as the girl walked forwards, Ash fell behind, out of her peripheral vision, and then moved sideways, towards the stairs.

Someone was in her way, moving too slowly for comfort. Ash couldn't push past him without drawing too much attention. But she couldn't stay here, because any second now the guards would—

"Stop right there!"

She froze.

"Have you seen a tour group around here?" she heard the girl ask.

"I said stop," the guard replied.

They were talking to the girl. They hadn't seen Ash. She overtook the guy in front of her as quickly as she dared, and then she was on the stairs.

It wouldn't take the guards long to realize the other girl wasn't the one they were looking for. When they did, they would lock down the building. Ash had no hope of making it to an exit before that happened.

She bit her lip. So how do I get out of here?

She could break a window and climb down, but all the windows were wall-sized, and in Ash's experience, the wider a pane of glass was, the harder it was to break – pressure got diffused across the surface, and big windows tended to be thicker. It would take her a while to smash one, and this building was full of people. Someone would stop her.

She was already getting a few strange looks as she walked around in her borrowed uniform. But no one openly questioned her – there were lots of weird outfits around, and several wandering employees had kids with them. One woman was even walking a dog through the halls. Ash guessed she didn't seem so strange by comparison.

A man in board shorts strolled past with a towel on his arm. Endless pools on the roof, Ash thought. There's roof access. Surely there'd be a fire escape or something. And even if there wasn't, swimming pools meant changing rooms, lockers, showers – lots of places to hide.

There was another flight of stairs up ahead. She ran up and opened the door at the top.

The roof was hot, bright and deserted. Ash could feel the concrete warming the soles of her shoes, and she smelled the chlorine from the pools, although she couldn't see them yet. A field of solar panels glinted around her. They would be generating lots of electricity today.

She ran across to the edge of the rooftop and looked down. A lone pedestrian waddled past far below. Not many people on this side of the building. Too high to jump – as expected – and there was no fire escape.

She circled the whole rooftop. No ladders, no external stairs, nothing. There were bridges to nearby buildings on the south-eastern and south-western sides, but they weren't accessible from the roof.

And what's more, there were no swimming pools. Just solar panels and blocky extractor fans. The roof was completely dry.

Ash was sure she'd heard the guide say there were pools on the roof. And she could still smell chlorine! So where were the pools?

She ran over to the eastern corner, following her nose. There – a glimpse of blue through the trees below. The two pools had their own separate building, too low and too far away to jump. As she watched, the man she'd seen in the board shorts climbed the stairs, dropped his towel and dived in. He'd been on his way *to* a swim, not from one.

Ash had cornered herself. She ran back to the door, hoping to backtrack down – and heard someone coming up the stairs. Someone *running*.

Fear squeezed her lungs. Security must know she was up here.

There was a fire axe in a glass case on the wall next to the door. She smashed the glass with her elbow, hefted the axe, crouched, and swung it like a baseball bat.

The blade slammed into the seam between the door and the ground like a giant doorstop. Seconds later, the handle turned. Someone was trying to get through.

The axe held. But the door wouldn't stay closed for long.

"Open up!" a voice demanded.

Choices. She could surrender, and hope there was a chance to escape before the cops showed up. Or she could jump and hope she didn't die.

She hated hoping. Anything that involved hoping was a bad plan.

Was there a third option?

Ash turned to the solar panels on the north-eastern side. A quick glance didn't discredit her crazy idea, so she moved closer.

Each row of connected panels was bolted to the ground at both ends. Standing between the three parallel grey strips, each tilted slightly to catch the most sun, Ash felt like she was standing on the head of a giant disposable razor.

She wished she had the Benji with her. It probably had a wrench in it somewhere – Benjamin seemed to have included just about everything else. Never mind, she thought. There'll be something around I can use.

There was a broom leaning against the wall – for sweeping leaves and debris off the panels, she guessed. She grabbed it and pulled off the head, exposing the square slot on the end.

The voice yelled, "Open this door!"

Got to hurry, Ash thought.

She ran back over to the panels. Using the slot in the broom handle, she twisted out the eight bolts pinning one of the solar arrays to the roof. But it was still connected by several power cables, which Ash wasn't sure how to cut. Electrocution on the roof of the Googleplex wasn't how she wanted to die.

She had to suppress a hysterical giggle when she thought of a group of police standing around her charred body, a pocket knife in her hand, the blade lodged in a cable. What in hell, one detective would ask another, was she trying to do?

She figured she could break the cables without touching them – the trick was leverage. She jammed the broom under the solar array, well away from the cables, and then heaved on the end, pulling upwards as sharply as she could.

There was a humming sound, and then a *snap!* The cables came loose, and the whole row of panels keeled over like synchronized swimmers. Photovoltaic cells chinked against the roof.

Ash dropped the broom, gripped the support poles under

the panel at one end of the row, and started dragging it towards the edge of the roof, inch by exhausting inch. She'd hoped the array would be lighter, having read somewhere that solar panels were more efficient if they were thin, or something like that.

But she could move it. That's what counted.

The noise of the array scraping along the concrete was like a stone door rumbling closed in a booby-trapped temple. Ash started listing all the movies with ancient temples in them, to distract herself from how far away the edge was, and how close the security guard sounded to breaking through the door.

Alien vs Predator, she thought. *Indiana Jones*, all four movies. *Tomb Raider*. Did *The Da Vinci Code* have one?

She reached the edge, moved to the other end of the row, and started pushing. The solar array poked out into the void, further and further.

It got easier as she neared halfway, since there was less resistance from the concrete. Two more shoves, Ash thought. That ought to do it.

She pressed her shoulder against the hot panel and pushed. One.

The row was sticking out over the edge of the rooftop like a bizarre work of modern art. Ash could feel it starting to see-saw.

She pushed again, harder. Two!

The row of panels took on a life of its own, lurching up out of her hands as the other end fell, sliding off the rooftop. There was an enormous clang and a splash as it hit the bottom of the unoccupied pool below, leaving Ash's end leaning against the roof at a crooked angle. She'd made a bridge to the pool building. The guy swimming stationary laps in the other pool didn't even seem to notice.

Do-it-yourself ramp, Ash thought. You will need: one broom, one rooftop, and several thousand dollars' worth of solar panels.

"What in God's name..."

Ash whirled around. There was a security guard standing in the doorway to the stairs, boggling at the mess she'd made.

"What..." he said. "What are you *doing*?"

Ash didn't answer. She threw herself onto the top panel, landing on her back, and immediately started sliding away from the rooftop, hurtling head first down the row of panels towards the pool.

It was like a water slide, but a million times more dangerous – there was nothing to stop her falling over the side and breaking her neck on the path below. She held her arms out sideways, keeping the panels between her elbows so she'd stay in the centre. She looked back the way she'd come, and saw the guard peering over the edge of the roof at her, astonished.

The sun blinded her, and she turned her eyes away. Trees were already appearing in her peripheral vision. I'm going to land head first, she thought. Got to slow down!

She squeezed the sides of the panels as she slid past, the hot metal burning her palms. She lost a little speed. Not enough.

She tried to swivel around so as she was falling feet first. But the panels were too slippery, and soon she was sliding sideways towards the edge. She was going to fall off.

"No!" she cried. She had to get back to the centre, or—

Splash! Suddenly she was underwater.

She'd made it. She was in the pool.

Choking, she fought the artificial current, and managed to plant her feet on the bottom. Her head breached the surface, and she gasped for air.

Blinking water out of her eyes, she turned around to see the security guard on the roof of Building 41, yelling into his radio.

No time to waste, she thought.

She clambered over the side and ran for the stairs, leaving damp shoe-prints on the concrete. She dashed down them three at a time. There was a rack of bikes nearby – she grabbed one and ran alongside it, gaining momentum, and then jumped on and pedalled towards the car park.

Now that she had no students to blend in with, the wet school uniform had outlived its usefulness as a disguise. Some of the employees wandering around the campus were already looking at her strangely, wondering why she was away from the group and riding a bike. And if security saw her, she was screwed. She had to get her clothes back.

She could see the school bus at the far end of the car park. The bicycle tyres hummed across the bitumen.

As she got close, she dismounted, dropped the bike, and ran around to the far side of the bus. Karen Sloven was standing in the shade, wearing Ash's clothes, and sucking on a cigarette.

"Where's the other half?" Karen asked.

For an alarming moment Ash thought she meant Benjamin, and wondered how she knew about him. Then she remembered the money.

"I want my clothes back first," she said.

"Why are you wet?"

"I went swimming. Clothes, please."

Karen shrugged, dropped her cigarette, stomped on it, and started undressing. Ash took off the green skirt and blazer, and passed them over. Karen handed her the jeans, shirt and jacket, which all now stank of cheap tobacco. Better wash that top, Ash thought, before Dad smells it.

She was annoyed at the inconvenience, but it wasn't a surprise. She had picked Karen because she was a smoker – a square bulge in her purse, teeth and fingernails slightly yellowed, gnawing on a pungent lump of gum. When the school group had just arrived and was still milling around the bus, Ash had approached her, figuring a poster girl for teenage rebellion was most likely to respond to her bizarre request. *I'll give you a hundred bucks to change clothes with me for an hour.*

Karen grimaced at the wet clothes. "I think I should get extra for this."

Ash pulled her clothes on, took a fifty and a twenty from the secret pocket inside the jacket's lining, and held them out. Karen took the money, and said, "Pleasure doing business with you," before taking another cigarette out of her purse and lighting it.

"Don't stay here too long," Ash said. "Go onto the campus and try to look lost. Otherwise they might realize you were never with the group."

"Unless you're offering me more money," Karen said, "I'll do what I want, thanks."

Ash rolled her eyes. She'd been trying to help, but if Karen wanted to get herself in more trouble, it really wasn't her problem. The worst Karen could tell anyone is that she'd met a teenage girl who wanted to see the inside of the Googleplex – no one would guess she was planning a rescue. They'd assume she was just a prankster, or a vandal.

Her phone was ringing. She turned away from the bus and started walking towards the road as she answered it.

A security guard saw her, looked her up and down, and moved on. He would be looking for a girl in uniform – she was safe.

"Yes?" she said.

"It's Hammond."

"Hi, Mr. Buckland. I've planted the bag—"

"We have to go," Buckland said. "Right now."

"What? Why?"

"Someone's made a new post on the Ghost's website. Something they want him to steal."

Ash frowned. "What does that have to do with anything?"

"It's Benjamin. Someone has sent the Ghost after Benjamin."

A Place to Hide

An icy fist closed around Ash's heart. Benjamin, she thought. Targeted by the Ghost.

"Why?" she demanded. "Why would somebody do that?"

"I'm not sure," Buckland said. "But the post is already an hour old. He could be very close already. We have to find somewhere for Benjamin to hide."

Ash grabbed her bike, the one she'd left outside the Googleplex when she arrived. She jumped on and started pumping the pedals, headed for the hotel they'd checked into. She said, "And then what? Just wait for him to give up?"

"He won't give up." Buckland's voice was grim. "He always gets what he wants."

"Then what can we do? How do we stop him?"

"We make sure we're the highest bidders."

Sweat erupted along Ash's brow. "Have you got enough?"

"I...I don't know."

"You don't *know*?"

"I can beat the current price, but it depends who wants him, and how badly."

This is crazy, Ash thought. People bidding on the life of my best friend.

"And if we win," she said, "then what? We just let the Ghost take him, and trust that he'll be returned alive?"

"The Ghost's smart. If he knows the buyer and the target are already together, he'll do nothing. It's not the first time something like this has happened."

"We need a safe house," Ash said. "We can't just wait on the street and hope that you've got the money to save us."

"There's an HBS International Bank on Castro Street," Buckland said. "I don't control it any more, since I'm legally dead, but I still know how to get you in. You can hide in the safe-deposit box vault – he'll never find you there. You'll be protected, at least until they unlock the vault in the morning."

"And what then?"

"I don't know, Ash! I'm thinking."

"How do I get to the bank from the Googleplex?"

"Um, head east on the Amphitheatre Parkway," Buckland said, "then south along North Shoreline Boulevard until you cross the Central Expressway, and then you're on Castro Street. It's about twenty minutes by bike."

"I'll see you in ten," Ash said, pedalling harder.

Eight minutes later she was screeching to a halt in front of HBS International, where Buckland was waiting with two large suitcases. He'd changed disguises – he now wore a pair of rimless glasses and a stick-on goatee. The bank loomed behind him, looking reassuringly solid.

I saw the guards vanish in the blink of an eye, the Ghost walk towards the wall, walk through *it, and walk back out.*

Ash shivered. "Where's Benjamin?" she asked.

"Hi, Ash," Benjamin whispered.

Ash looked around. "Where are—" Her gaze fell on one of the suitcases, which looked more full than the other. "Oh, I get it."

"Don't look at it," Buckland said. "I don't think he could have found us yet, but we can't be too careful."

Ash raised her eyes. "And how is Benjamin being in there going to protect him? Is that a bulletproof suitcase?"

"It's going to get you two into the vault for the night." Buckland lifted the empty suitcase. "This one's yours."

"Damn, Benjamin," Ash said. "How did you get us into this?"

"I have no idea," he said miserably.

They walked to a secluded park around the corner, Buckland dragging Benjamin's suitcase behind him. The wheels rumbled along the pavement.

They stood in the shade of a sprawling tree, invisible to anybody behind the windows of the surrounding skyscrapers, or watching through one of the hundreds of satellites that whirled around the earth. Ash looked around. There were a few people in the park, but no one appeared to be looking her way.

She dropped the suitcase, unzipped it, stepped in, and curled into a ball. She felt Buckland shut the lid above her and zip it closed. Claustrophobia arose immediately, despite the flexibility and porousness of the material. She sucked in a few deep breaths and felt a little better.

There was something large and hard and flat inside the lid, shaped like a small tabletop. Maybe Ash's guess about bulletproof suitcases hadn't been too far off.

The case lurched up, and started to roll across the grass. Ash realized that Buckland must be dragging both her and Benjamin, and felt a rush of gratitude. The original agreement had been that he would give them the hit list, and they would give him ten per cent of the rewards. Flying them both to

California, purchasing Benjamin from a thief, and lugging them both around in suitcases was more than he'd signed on for.

Assuming, of course, that that was what he was doing. Ash felt her chest tighten. Would Buckland really spend all his money saving Benjamin from the Ghost? What if he was just saying he would? What if he saw an opportunity in this? He could sell Benjamin to the Ghost, or to the buyer, or use him as bait to lure the Ghost out and get his emerald back...

Where was he taking them? Surely the bank wasn't this far away.

Ash wondered if she could get out of the suitcase. The tag for the zip was on the outside, but maybe she could get a pin out of her watch and use that, or just stretch the fabric until it tore. Buckland could probably overpower her, but they were still on Castro Street, where there'd be lots of people to hear her scream.

The angle changed; the suitcase was rolling up a ramp. Ash tried to remember if HBS International had had stairs. Where are we going? she thought.

She heard some automatic doors slide open and closed. A voice said, "How can I help you today?"

"Hi, my name's Henry Bridges," Buckland said. "I called earlier about opening a safe-deposit box? I know the bank's about to close, but—"

"Certainly, sir," the woman said. "I'll just need to see some ID."

"No problem."

Ash felt relieved, then guilty. Her faith in Hammond Buckland had collapsed after only minutes of discomfort.

Maybe he's trapping us here so the Ghost can get us, she thought. And then she realized that was hardly reassuring.

"Right this way, sir."

"Thank you."

The suitcase started to move again. Ash had been in several HBS banks since Buckland's "death", and each one had had a framed picture of Buckland on the wall next to the counter. It's impressive, she thought, that a pair of glasses and a fake beard is enough to stop the receptionist from recognizing him.

"Just here, Mr. Bridges. Push the buzzer when you're done."

"Thank you."

Ash heard something large and heavy clank closed, and then Buckland unzipped the suitcases. Light poured in. "Okay, guys, you can come out now."

Ash sat up, tilting her head from side to side, loosening her neck and joints. Most safe-deposit box vaults she'd been in had resembled post offices, the walls gridded with safes the size of shoeboxes. But this vault looked more like a high-school locker room. The boxes were tall and wide, designed to hold art as well as cash.

There must be so much money in this room, she thought. Then she caught herself. Most of it was probably where it belonged.

"Aren't there cameras?" she asked.

"We're in a blind spot," Buckland said. "But it's visible from the door, so you'll have to set up those mirrors before the woman comes back."

The flat object in the suitcase made sense now. Ash unzipped a compartment in the lid to reveal a mirror, brand new, the surface dulled by protective plastic. Ash stood it up in the corner at a forty-five degree angle between two perpendicular rows of boxes.

"It's not tall enough," she said.

"I've got one too," Benjamin said, removing an identical mirror from his suitcase. "We can put one on top of the other."

Seeing him for the first time since learning of the threat, Ash noticed how shaken he looked. He kept rubbing his sweaty hands on his jeans, and the tiny mole on his cheek, normally a cheery pink, had gone white.

"You okay?" she asked.

"I'm fine," he said.

They propped up the two mirrors, creating a triangle of

floor space in which they would be invisible, and huddled behind them.

"I'll come back for you in the morning," Buckland said. "Hopefully I'll have managed to outbid everyone else by then."

"What if you haven't?" Ash asked.

There was a dark look in Buckland's eyes. "Then we'll have to find another way out," he said. "Maybe we can find the top bidder and...*persuade* him or her to contribute to our bid."

"So what do Ash and I do?" Benjamin asked. "Just sit here?"

"If I were you," Buckland said, "I'd spend the time figuring out who wants you, and why."

"I've been trying," Benjamin said. "I don't know!"

"Try harder," Buckland said, and pushed the buzzer.

Ash heard the door unlock and the woman come in. "Is everything to your satisfaction, Mr. Bridges?" she asked.

"Perfect," Buckland said. "Thank you very much."

Ash heard Buckland's footsteps retreat out the door. The woman stayed.

Has she noticed the mirror? Ash wondered. Can she tell we're here?

The woman's heels clicked away, and the door closed. The lights in the vault flickered off, pitching the space into darkness.

* * *

The house was ordinary. Boring, even. Cheap and small in a cheap and small neighbourhood. It was so unremarkable that Peachey could hardly believe his eyes.

Ashley Arthur can't live here, he thought. No way. Whoever she is, she's got resources – money, equipment, intel. She has major backing from major players. What would she be doing in a place like this?

It had to be a fake address. He'd wasted his time coming here.

Either that, said a voice in his head, or you were beaten by a poor, everyday teenager.

Peachey clenched his teeth. He didn't have anything else to go on. If Ashley wasn't living here, he might have to abandon hope of finding her and go after Buckland some other way.

I need to know for certain, he thought. He walked up to the door and pushed the bell.

He heard it ring inside.

He waited.

No one came.

There was a security screen door in front of the main one, so he couldn't use a credit card or a knife to get inside. But a door is only as strong as its hinges. Peachey picked up a rock from the garden with the intention of cracking them open—

—and saw a key on the ground.

Spare key under a rock? he thought. Seriously? This can't be the place.

He went inside anyway.

The house was cramped and dark, the curtains closed. He stood still just inside the door, gun drawn, and listened.

No voices, no scuffling, no breathing. Ashley, or whoever lived here, wasn't home.

He wandered through the house, looking at the old books and the small TV and the battered tables and shelves. The couch was scarred by cat claws, but the house had no litter tray or food bowl, probably meaning that the furniture was second-hand.

He soon found a bedroom that looked like it belonged to a teenage girl. The bed was short and narrow, there was a stack of textbooks on the dresser. A lava lamp gurgled in the corner. Peachey opened the wardrobe and found a row of jeans and tank tops folded on shelves.

But something about the space struck him as artificial. No posters covered the walls, advertising romantic comedies or pop singers or heart-throbs. No novels lined the bookshelves – it was all non-fiction, mostly history and popular science. There were no speakers to attach to an mp3 player or radio.

Peachey was looking at the room of a very serious – perhaps even sad – girl.

Who cares? he thought. The point is, it's empty. So do I wait for Ashley or whoever to come back, or is there something here I can use to find out where she is?

He didn't like the idea of waiting. Sooner or later the phone he'd been given would ring, and he'd be asked to go somewhere and do something. His mysterious benefactors probably wouldn't respond well if he said, Sorry, I'm busy at a stakeout. I'll kill your target once I'm done here, okay?

And it wouldn't just be a matter of enduring some harsh words. They would want to punish him. They'd track him down using his phone, follow him here, and he'd have to—

Wait. Back up. Track him down using his phone.

I can track Ashley using her phone, he realized. If I can find the number.

He went out into the kitchen, where the landline phone was sitting on its charger. There was no address book near it, so he scrolled through the list of recently dialled numbers. There were two mobile numbers which appeared several times – probably the occupants of the house calling one another. Peachey grabbed a pen and wrote them on his hand.

He'd seen a computer in the other bedroom, which he guessed belonged to a single middle-aged man. The bed was longer, but still narrow. A flannel shirt and some corduroy trousers were crumpled on the floor. There were some novels on the shelves this time, mostly ageing crime fiction. There were some books about computers and web design as well, some instructional, some historical. When Peachey had entered the room before, he'd just been checking that it was empty. Now that he was looking more closely he noticed the picture frames on the bedside table, atop the bookshelves, mounted on the walls.

Almost all of the pictures were of Ashley Arthur.

I'm in the right place, he thought.

Many of the pictures also featured an older man – probably the occupant of the room, possibly Ashley's father. Glasses, greying hair, a vague *Where was I?* smile.

One of the frames was face down on the dresser. Peachey picked it up. It was a snapshot of a woman who looked similar enough to Ashley to be her mother or her aunt. She looked vaguely familiar to Peachey, like maybe he'd seen her on TV or been served by her at a restaurant, but the exact memory eluded him, so he put it back down.

The computer looked old, but booted up quickly – the insides might be newer than the shell. No password. Peachey opened the web browser, went to Google®, and typed *how to track a mobile phone*.

He knew there was a service called Google® Latitude that allowed users to see the locations of their friends (or their friends' phones) but that required permission. Instead, he scrolled down until he found something called SpouseCatchers.

He clicked the link and scanned the splash page. *Is your wife or husband acting strangely? Coming and going at odd hours? No need to hire a PI – track their phone.*

Perfect, he thought.

He typed in the numbers from the credit card he'd been given. There was a disclaimer on the site that said SpouseCatchers would bear no responsibility for misuse of the service, and that tracing someone's phone without their consent was a violation of the Surveillance Devices Act which could result in two years' imprisonment or a $26,000 fine.

Isn't the lack of permission the whole point? Peachey wondered. He clicked *I accept*, and was in.

The first phone number he tried produced a Google® map with an arrow pointing at a spot not far from the house. It was the HQ of a web-design company. Peachey thought of the computing books and figured that the number probably belonged to Ashley's father, and that he was at work.

Peachey tried the second number. Another map came up. Mountain View, California. What the hell?

The arrow pointed to a bank – HBS International. Hammond Buckland's bank, Peachey thought. What a surprise.

He wrote down the address and was halfway through

booking a plane ticket when his phone buzzed. His benefactors must have noticed the activity on his credit card already.

It was a text message: *Michael. How are you enjoying your freedom?*

Peachey raised an eyebrow. Not the tone he'd expected. He typed, *Wondering who to thank.* Then he hit *send*.

The reply came almost instantly. The messages were probably being typed on a computer rather than a phone. *Soon. After you do a little favour for me.*

Me, not us. Was he talking to the boss? Peachey replied, *What favour?*

Again, the reply was immediate. *I need you to go to California and protect something that belongs to me.*

Peachey didn't believe in coincidence. *Where exactly?*

The Googleplex, in Mountain View. Interested?

Curiouser and curiouser. Peachey smiled. *On my way*, he wrote.

Detective Wright's fists were white around the steering wheel. His nose was broken. A river of blood, hot and wet, was dribbling down his chin and soaking his collar.

He didn't wipe it off. In fact, he barely noticed it. An ion-storm of firing synapses was raging in his skull.

Got to get to the airport, he thought. Got to beat Peachey.

It wasn't about anger and it wasn't about earning his salary. As long as he'd been a cop, Wright had been addicted to the feeling he got every time he put away a killer or drug lord or arms dealer. There was a strong sense of rightness, that he'd made the world safer. Better. There was a place for bad guys: prison. And there was a place for good guys: everywhere else. His job was to make sure everybody was where they belonged.

Every now and again a jury let someone go when they shouldn't have, or a parole board released somebody too early, and that bothered him. But this was far worse. This time, a bad guy had just *walked out* the goddamn front gate of Hallett State. That felt more wrong than anything else he could imagine.

And Peachey was a very bad guy. Wright's first experience of him had been the sight of a severed hand lying in an alleyway. The first time he'd actually seen him in the flesh, he was blowing the brains out the back of Hammond Buckland's head.

No one was going to stop Wright from putting Peachey back in his cell. For good, this time.

A car honked at him as he roared past – the driver apparently hadn't noticed the police light he'd put on the roof. He ignored her, swerving left and screeching up the ramp onto the highway.

He had no proof that Peachey was catching a plane anywhere. But after breaking into a police station and killing a SWAT cop, it made no sense to hang around. And when every officer in the state knew his face, he wouldn't feel safe driving.

The airport nearest the station had been locked down the minute Peachey's escape had become public. Standard protocol. No flights out. But Wright was driving further. He figured Peachey wouldn't use the nearest airport – he'd try to trick them.

It was a lot of speculation. But, Wright thought, I was right about him shaving his head, wasn't I?

Nobody else thought Peachey would try to fly out. Too much security. You needed money, you needed ID, and you had to ditch your weapons. There were easier ways to get out of town.

But Peachey hadn't escaped on his own, Wright knew. *No one* breaks out of Hallett State – you leave when your time is up. Someone was helping him, and anyone with that kind of power could procure a fake passport and a ceramic weapon that wouldn't show up in the metal detector.

The traffic was too heavy. He wasn't moving fast enough. He drove up onto the shoulder and floored the accelerator, siren howling.

His phone was ringing. He snapped it open. "What?"

"Detective Wright, this is Agent Gerritz. Where are you?"

"On my way to the airport," Wright said. "Have you caught him?"

"No. We need you to come back to the station so we can—"

Wright hung up. They wanted to interview him about what had happened at the police station. They would ask him the same questions over, and over, and over, while Peachey was getting on a plane and escaping for ever.

He was getting closer. More and more taxis were falling behind as he sped past.

The phone rang again. He ignored it.

I'll go back to the station, all right, he thought. Dragging Michael Peachey by his treacherous throat.

The airport was a bright oasis in the gloom of the surrounding fields. A 737 swept overhead, impossibly big this close to the runway.

Wright screeched to a halt in the taxi rank, grabbed his Colt out of the holster, and got out. A cab driver pounded on the horn. Wright ignored him.

He ran through the sliding glass doors marked *Departures*, past the ads for luxury cars and investment companies, and then he was in the airport, already scanning the jet-lagged faces of every bald person he saw.

Too tall.

Too fat.

Female.

A voice above him said, "This is the final boarding call for passengers on flight QF107 to San José, California. All passengers for this flight please make your way to gate 17." He ignored it.

A teenage boy saw his gun, and said, "Whoa! Take it easy, man." Other people were starting to look over, cry out, back away.

He kept looking. Too many tattoos. Chin too wide—

"Hey!"

Wright turned. An airport cop was pointing her gun at him. "Drop your weapon!" she roared.

Wright exhaled, a mist of blood bursting from his shattered nose. "I'm a cop," he said.

"Put the goddamn gun down," the woman said.

Wright lowered the gun slowly. "Take it easy." He gestured with his free hand towards his jacket. "I'm reaching for my badge."

"Drop the gun first," she replied.

Wright was about to comply. Then he looked over the cop's shoulder – and saw Peachey.

He'd already gone through the security checkpoint. He was standing at the bottom of the escalator to the departure lounge, staring incredulously at Wright.

"Peachey!" Wright yelled.

Peachey smiled, took one step backwards, and began to rise out of sight.

Wright whipped the gun back up, took aim at Peachey's heart, and squeezed the trigger.

Blam!

It was like getting kicked in the chest. The gun tumbled from Wright's fingers.

The airport cop fired a second time. This shot missed the Kevlar armour, punching through Wright's shoulder. He felt a ligament rip and heard a gurgling sound as blood sprayed up into his ear.

"Damn it," he wheezed. The world was starting to spin. "He's getting...he's going to..."

The carpet rushed up to meet him. He tried to push the ground away. Failed. Not enough blood getting to his brain.

He kept one eye open long enough to see the cop's shoes approaching at a bizarre angle. "Control," she was saying. "The situation has been resolved."

It's not resolved! Wright thought. He's escaping! He's... I can't...

He blacked out.

Behind the airport cop, Peachey was riding the escalator up, up and away.

* * *

"Well," Benjamin said. "This sucks."

"Yep," Ash said.

They were sitting on the floor in the blind spot under the camera, their backs against the deposit boxes. The only illumination was a blinking green light on the underside of the camera, which barely punctured the blackness. They'd taken down the mirrors, but Ash couldn't see the rest of the vault. She couldn't even see Benjamin's face, or her own hands.

Given the dark, they might well have been free to move around. But the camera could have a night-vision function, or a motion sensor that would turn on the lights. It wasn't worth the risk.

Ash's stomach growled.

"What the hell was that?" Benjamin demanded, alarmed.

"I'm hungry," Ash said.

"Oh. Sorry." She felt him press a muesli bar into her hand.

"Thanks. How many more of these do we have?"

"That's the last one."

They hadn't had many, but that was probably for the best. No toilet in a bank vault, Ash reflected.

"You want to share it?" she asked.

"It's fine."

She tore into the wrapper, feeling guilty. Whatever this was, it was certainly her fault. Benjamin would be a straight-laced, law-abiding choirboy if it weren't for her. He had followed her into crime the way a puppy follows whoever fills its bowl, and now, maybe, he was going to die because of it. *And* she was eating the last muesli bar.

But he'd said he didn't want any and she was hungry. It was his choice. She couldn't force him to eat it any more than she could have stopped him trailing her down the dangerous road she'd chosen.

She looked at the glowing hands of her watch. Just after eleven. They'd been crouched in the darkness for seven hours, and they still had ten to go.

Right now, she thought, Dad would be at work, finishing the salmon sandwich he always packs for lunch. What will he think when he gets home and I'm not there? How long can I pretend to be at a friend's house? To make things worse, she had no idea what would happen when the vault door opened. Would Buckland come in, triumphant, having bought Benjamin or manipulated the other bidder? Or would the Ghost be there, a terrible grin on his lips, ready to make Benjamin disappear in a puff of smoke?

"What about your mum?" she asked. "Has she won the lotto or something? Taking you would be a good way to get to her."

Benjamin sighed. "She would have told me, and I would have told you. I tell you everything."

"I know. Just asking."

They had been over every possible reason someone could want him, alive or dead. Money. Revenge. Love. ("If they wanted a date, they could have just asked me," Benjamin had said.) But they had found nothing convincing. For all his talents, Benjamin was no more desirable as a prisoner than any other teenage boy.

Ash finished the muesli bar and tucked the wrapper into her pocket. She stared into the inky shadows. "Care for a game of I Spy?"

Benjamin chortled. The sound was refreshing. "You think of that joke just now?"

"A while ago," she admitted. "I wanted to save it for the halfway mark, when we'd need it most."

"We halfway already?"

"No. I got impatient."

Benjamin laughed again. "Have I ever told you that there's no one on earth I'd rather be trapped in a pitch-black, cold, scary safe-deposit box vault with than you?"

"Don't think it's ever come up," Ash said.

"Well, it's true." He cleared his throat. "I spy with my little eye something beginning with D."

"Dark."

"Correct."

"I spy with my little eye," Ash said, "something beginning with B."

"Blackness."

"Correct. You are a worthy foe."

They played a few more rounds, but after shadow, dimness and gloom, they ran out of synonyms. Ash tried "aphotic", but Benjamin said the words in I Spy had to be nouns, not adjectives.

After a few minutes of silence, she put her hand over his and squeezed. He squeezed back.

"Did Buckland tell you we screwed up?" he asked.

"What? When?"

"At the library. That hard drive you took wasn't the one on the hit list – it wasn't big enough."

"It did look too small to hold four terabytes," Ash said. "So what was on it?"

"Indexing software, with about a million files."

"So…we stole the city library's catalogue?"

"Yeah."

"Whoops. I wonder how we can return that without getting busted."

"Could be harder than it was stealing it."

Ash sighed. They weren't even that good at their jobs. How had they become important enough to end up in this mess?

"Let's talk about the Ghost," Benjamin said suddenly.

Ash was startled. "Why?"

"I want to work out how he stole Buckland's emerald. I'll feel safer here once I know for certain he can't walk through walls."

That makes sense, Ash thought. "What if," she began, "the emerald Buckland put in the vault was actually a duplicate made from coloured ice? It would have melted on its own, without the Ghost needing to go anywhere near it."

"Buckland said it was the real deal."

"He said it wasn't a hologram. How do you tell cleanly cut ice from a gemstone?"

"It would have left water on the floor when it melted."

"Dry ice, then. Buckland wouldn't have noticed a little bit of CO_2 in the air, right?"

"Maybe not," Benjamin said doubtfully. "But I think he would have noticed he was carrying around a block of ice instead of a priceless emerald."

Ash sighed. "Probably."

"Sorry."

There was a pause.

"What about the steel bricks?" Ash said. "The ones Buckland made his vault out of. Did he say where he got them?"

"Don't think so. Why?"

"But it only took sixty-six of them to build the whole thing, right? So they must have been really big. What if one was hollow?"

"Wait." Benjamin sounded excited. "Are you suggesting the Ghost intercepted the bricks on their way to Buckland, and sealed himself *inside* one?"

"Yes," Ash said. "Along with some cutting equipment and an oxygen tank. Once the vault's been built, he cuts his way out, steals the emerald, and welds himself back in. From the outside, the vault looks exactly the same."

Benjamin said nothing. But the more Ash thought about it, the more she was sure that it couldn't have happened any other way. "He closes bidding on the site using his phone," she continued, "prompting Buckland to cut a hole in the wall so he can check on his emerald – and after he's gone, *that's* the Ghost's escape route! It's perfect!"

"Impressive."

"Yeah. I can't—" Ash paused.

That hadn't sounded like Benjamin's voice.

"Benjamin?" she said.

Silence.

She lifted his hand. It was limp in her fingers. Her heart kicked in her chest.

"*Benjamin?*"

There was a noise behind her. A swish and a clank – the sound of a deposit box being closed. One of the big ones.

The Ghost has been in here with us the whole time, she thought. Just like with the bricks.

Ash knew she should be doing something to defend herself, but she couldn't bear not knowing what had happened to her best friend.

She whipped out her phone, and pointed the glowing screen at Benjamin. His eyes had rolled backwards into his head, and his jaw was stretched open in a silent scream.

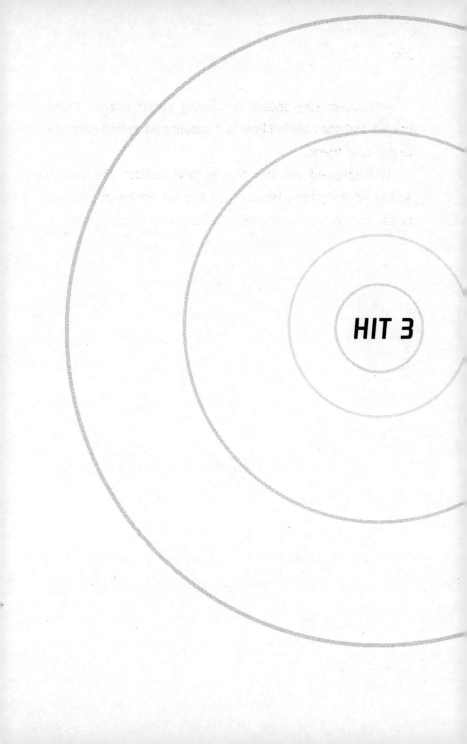

HIT 3

My Enemy's Enemy

Ash choked on a hiccup of pure terror. "No!" She shook Benjamin's shoulders – had he fainted? Was he *dead*?

Please, she thought. I'll give up thieving, I'll go on a date with you, I'll do anything, just please, Benjamin, don't be dead. There was something sticking out of his neck. A knife. No, too small. It was a syringe, or a dart perhaps.

Maybe he's alive, Ash told herself, desperate. He's no good to anyone if he's not, right? The Ghost wouldn't kill him. Maybe he's just unconscious.

Footsteps. Someone was drawing closer behind her, and

she couldn't afford to ignore them any longer. She turned, stood, listened. Tried to judge his position, so she could dodge him when he attacked.

And then what? Dance around him for the next nine and a half hours, hoping Buckland would come to the rescue when the bank opened?

"You're making a mistake," she said.

The steps kept coming.

"Seriously." Her voice shook. "Don't do this. Benjamin is worth more alive, and free, than whatever you're being paid."

She listened. There was silence.

He's interested, she thought.

"Great," she said. "Now give me the antidote to whatever you've drugged him with. Then we can talk about this."

She glanced back at Benjamin, and saw that he was gone. He had been taken without the slightest sound.

"No!" she cried. "Don't leave! I'm serious! There's a woman trapped in the Googleplex, and Benjamin's the only one who can hack the security system to get to her, and—"

Something clicked in her brain. Whoa, she thought. That's it!

"That's why someone put a bounty on him!" she said. "Whoever imprisoned the girl hired you to take out Benjamin before he could rescue her. So whatever they're paying you for this, Alice must be worth more! Way more!"

Her guts wrenched at the realization that she was sacrificing Alice to save Benjamin. But it was the only way. She'd find a way to save Alice from the Ghost later. She just needed time.

"Please," she said. "Don't take him. We can work this out."

Crack.

The room filled with an other-worldly red glow. Ash saw the Ghost, tall and cold-eyed, Benjamin slung over his shoulder like a roll of carpet. Like he weighed nothing.

Ash's eyes widened. It couldn't be true.

"Liam? *You're* the Ghost?"

The boy from the dance dropped the glow stick to the floor. "Tell me about Alice," he said.

"Thank you. Enjoy your evening. Goodbye! Thanks. Enjoy your stay. Thank you. Goodbye!"

Peachey nodded politely to the beaming flight attendant as he disembarked, the last in a very long line of passengers. He looked out over San José as he walked down the steps to the tarmac. The city lights sparkled like those of an old pinball machine.

He straightened his legs, stretched his neck, blinked his dried-up eyes. It had been a long flight.

His job had always required an unpleasant amount of travel. There were few countries he'd never been to. Anywhere there are people, he thought, there will be someone who wants someone else dead.

For this reason, airports and hotels and hire-car stands no longer interested him – he could sleepwalk through them. As he strolled through the arrivals gate, threading through the clusters of sleepy passengers, only a small part of him was wondering whether to rent a car to get to the Googleplex, which would leave a paper trail, or take a taxi, which would create video evidence of his trip and possibly a body to dispose of, depending on the inquisitiveness of the driver, or ride a bus, which would require him to find a stop and a timetable and be near poor people, which was always an unpleasant reminder of his childhood in the Solomon Islands.

A small part of his brain was calculating all this, but the rest was pondering a larger question – why was he being sent to the Googleplex in the first place?

We need you to go to California and protect something that belongs to us.

He was a hit man, not a security guard. His employer wouldn't have gone to the trouble of breaking him out of prison just to have him look after something. So Peachey must also be required to kill somebody.

But who? Why?

The text messages had felt formal – no typos, no abbreviations, correct grammar. This led Peachey to believe that he'd been communicating with someone old, someone who hadn't grown up with the text-talk that saturated modern culture. Probably a woman, like most of his clients – women were less likely to kill than men, but in his experience, they were more likely to outsource the job.

So, he thought. I'm looking for an old woman who owns something in California. Or I'm being manipulated, in which case it could be a young boy who has nothing but a mobile phone and an unusual amount of influence in the prison system.

Peachey decided to rent a car, rationalizing that the paperwork would only lead to the false identity that had been created for him. He didn't want the staff to see the wad of cash, so he took it out, removed six fifty-dollar notes, and returned it to his pocket. He put the notes in his wallet as he approached the hire-car stand.

"Hi there," said a man behind the counter. He peered at Peachey through thick glasses that made his eyes cartoonishly large.

"Hello," Peachey said. "I'd like a car for tonight and tomorrow."

The man took out a catalogue and Peachey selected the most generic-looking sedan he could find.

"Excellent choice," the man said.

He took Peachey's fake name, address and phone number and typed them all into his computer, and then said, "That'll be two hundred and sixty-three dollars, please."

Peachey took out his wallet and handed over the six fifties, pleased that his estimate had been so close. The man passed him his change and the keys.

Peachey asked, "Could I have a map as well?"

"There's a GPS navigator in the car," the man said proudly.

Which would record destinations. "I don't like those fancy new gadgets," Peachey said. "A paper map would be great."

The man put a disposable map on the desk and held a pen over it. "Where you headed?" he asked.

Peachey said, "Los Gatos." That was in the opposite direction to Mountain View, but about the same distance from the airport. Should anyone check how much petrol was in the tank when he returned the car, it would match up.

The man drew two circles on the map, one for the airport and one for Los Gatos, and handed it over. "See you later!" he said.

"Thanks."

Peachey walked out to the pick-up area, clicked the keys, and heard a car chirp nearby. He found the car, got in, started the engine, and pulled out of the car park.

He was supposed to await further instructions once he got here. There was little point breaking into the Googleplex when he didn't know what he was supposed to be protecting. But there was no harm in driving out there and waiting nearby. When the phone rang, he would be ready to go.

The highway was almost empty at this time of night. A handful of cabs whizzed past him, headed back towards the airport. He drove carefully, slow enough that he didn't need to overtake anybody, fast enough that nobody overtook him. You never knew what people would remember when they got home. He was a forgettable man driving a forgettable-looking car, but there was no sense being reckless.

Peachey flicked on the radio, which was tuned to some classical station, like every other rental car he'd ever been in. He kept pushing *seek* until he found a modern hard-rock tune. That felt more appropriate for a midnight journey towards murder. The soundtrack of his life was important to him.

He passed a sign that said *Welcome to Mountain View*, and smiled.

"But," Ash said, "but...you're a kid."

Liam, or whoever he was, remained silent. He'd said nothing since that first quiet order. *Tell me about Alice.*

"How can *you* be the Ghost?" she demanded. "You're barely older than us!"

He said nothing.

Ash knew she'd done things some people would call impossible for a girl her age. She shouldn't have thought she was the only one.

But she'd seen the looks on the faces of the soldiers in the mine – could that much fear really have been caused by a teenager?

"What were you doing at my school dance? Who sent you?"

His face was unreadable in the dark. After a pause, he flexed the fingers of his right hand, slowly, strangely – and suddenly a knife appeared in his grasp.

Ash stared. How had he done that?

"Tell me," the Ghost said, "which is Benjamin's dominant eye?"

He pressed the tip of the blade against Benjamin's face. A drop of blood welled up at his tear duct and fell down his cheek.

"No!" Ash cried.

The Ghost paused. "Then tell me about Alice."

"Okay," Ash said. Her fists clenched at her sides. "Okay. Just put him down. I'll tell you everything I know."

He dropped Benjamin to the floor with a thud. Ash winced.

"I don't know her age, her last name, or how long she's been held captive," Ash said. "But because you're here, I know she's very important to someone, and I know she's being held in the Googleplex, at coordinates, um…" Concentrate, she told herself. "Thirty-seven point four two one five, and negative one twenty-two point zero eight five five. She has access to a fax machine, or did, within the past few weeks. I don't think Google® knows she's there."

There was a long silence.

It's not enough, she thought wildly. He's changing his mind!

"Alice," the Ghost said thoughtfully, like he wasn't sure he was pronouncing it right. Then he started to laugh, a quiet chuckling that reverberated around the vault until Ash felt like she was surrounded by giggling demons.

He stopped abruptly. "Okay," he said. "Let's rescue Alice." He pointed at Benjamin. "He can get us in?"

"He can get us through the electronic locks in the building. But as for the guards and cameras—"

She broke off. What would the Ghost do to the guards?

"We'll just try and avoid those," she said.

He replied, "You're not coming."

"What?"

Silence.

"You think you can just leave me here?"

"I don't need you," he said. "You've told me what I need to know."

It was true. Ash wasn't sure what to say.

"You'd be dead right now," the Ghost said, "except that you're my leverage over him."

He kicked Benjamin's chest.

Ash recoiled as though it were she who'd been hit. "You're a sociopath," she whispered.

He was flexing his hand again, twisting loops into the air. Suddenly there was a gun in it. More sleight of hand.

"I'm sorry," Ash said, alarmed. "I didn't mean to make you mad."

"You didn't," the Ghost said, and then he shot her.

She fell to the floor, startled – tried to throw her arms back, protect her spine, but her limbs were already stiffening up. It was like there was ice in her arteries, spreading out from the dart jammed into her flesh, freezing her in place.

She screamed, but it came out as a choked groan. She couldn't move, couldn't even blink – and suddenly she couldn't breathe.

He injects them with a tiny amount of tetrodotoxin, which
   paralyses them
     stops the breathing
      lowers the body temperature
       slows the pulse down until it's undetectable

Tetrodotoxin, Ash thought. He's going to bury me alive, and turn me into a zombie!

She couldn't shift her gaze, but she could see the Ghost moving in her peripheral vision. He was bending over Benjamin, holding something – A blade? A syringe? – and then he brought it down, a quick stab to the sternum.

Ash tried to shout, No! You stay away from him! But her lips wouldn't budge. She still couldn't breathe. She couldn't *breathe*!

Benjamin choked and spluttered and gasped.

"Get up," the Ghost said.

"Just a minute," Benjamin wheezed. "Give me a minute."

"You're fine. Get up."

Ash saw Benjamin stagger to his feet. He's okay, she thought.

"You understand the deal?" the Ghost said.

He was awake, Ash realized. He was awake the whole time, listening, but frozen, like I am now.

"Your deal sucks," Benjamin said. "We're changing it."

The Ghost lashed out so fast that Ash barely saw it happen. There was a sharp *crack*, and suddenly Benjamin was on his knees, spitting a gob of blood to the floor.

"I'm sorry," the Ghost said. "I didn't catch that."

Benjamin, do what he says, Ash thought. Please.

"Ash comes with us," Benjamin said. "Or I won't get you in."

Smack! Ash saw it this time – a brutal fist, slashing down through the air towards Benjamin's skull. He tumbled backwards, teeth bared.

"Pardon me?" the Ghost said. "I still can't hear you."

"Then open your goddamn ears!" Benjamin howled. "I won't help you without Ash!"

He was out of Ash's line of sight now, but she saw the Ghost kick him. The sound was like a sledgehammer hitting a dead pig. She heard the air rush out of Benjamin's lungs.

The Ghost stared down at his captive. After a long moment, he said, "Once you accept you have no control, this will be much easier. You must realize I can do worse things to you."

"And they won't make any difference," Benjamin said, breathing heavily. "Because nothing could be worse than being separated from Ash. So you've either got to kill me, or accept that she's coming with us. And I'm no good to you dead."

The Ghost said nothing.

"Wake her up," Benjamin said.

Ash's lungs were on fire. How long have I got, she wondered, before the lack of oxygen gives me brain damage?

She told herself that Benjamin had been paralysed for longer than this, and he seemed okay. It didn't help.

The Ghost approached her, a needle in his hand. "Fine," he said. "She comes with us."

He paused, the needle hovering above Ash's chest.

Hurry up! she thought. I can't breathe!

"But ask yourself this," the Ghost said. "How far can you push me before I decide you'd be less trouble with your tongue cut out?"

He stabbed Ash in the heart.

It felt like a billion volts straight to her core. She screamed, her arms shuddering by her sides, the back of her skull thudding against the floor.

Benjamin was at her side in an instant, pushing the Ghost out of the way. "Ash," he said, grabbing her hand. "It's okay."

She'd inhaled a lot of saliva in her first gasp of air, and now she was choking on it. She coughed, the moisture crackling in her lungs.

Her breathing steadied, and Benjamin hugged her tightly.

She whispered in his ear, "How are we going to get out of this?"

"I have no idea," he replied.

The Dead of Night

Detective Wright opened his eyes.

As a child he'd bought a mask of Frankenstein's monster for Halloween, and had discovered it was too big – even with the elastic, it kept slipping down his face until he couldn't see through the eyeholes. To solve the problem, he baked the mask in his parents' oven to soften the plastic and then he put it on, taping the edges to his skin and squeezing the nose onto his own with clothes pegs, hoping the mask would harden in the shape of his face.

In the burn unit at the hospital, a doctor had told his

parents that the clothes pegs probably saved his life, preventing him from inhaling the fumes from the hot polyester.

Now he wondered why he was wearing the hot mask and the pegs again. Surely his mother had thrown it out? Then he touched his face and realized that he wasn't wearing it – it just seemed like he was. His broken nose felt hot and pinched.

He tried to sit up, and suddenly the rest of his body felt the same way. His ribs seemed to be crushing his torso, and his shoulder ached for some reason.

I was shot, he thought. By that airport cop. I remember now.

"You're awake."

A guy who didn't look like a doctor or a nurse was sitting by the bed. He was in a dark uniform – a cop? A security guard? Scanning the area, Wright saw that he was in some kind of sick bay. Not a hospital. Too small, too limited.

"What time is it?" he croaked.

The uniformed guy pointed at the clock on the wall. Wright groaned. He'd been unconscious for hours. Peachey could be anywhere by now.

"You're in a lot of trouble," the guy said. "Detective or not, you can't just go waving your gun around at an airport."

"It was an emergency. It still is. Where am I?"

"Oh, about..." The guy thought about it. "Twenty, maybe thirty metres from where you got shot. Some of your colleagues are here to pick you up, but the doc said she's got to talk to you first. Check your head. I reckon she might find it tough, since you were clearly already crazy."

"Go get her," Wright said. "And the cops. Get them all in here."

The guy left, too slowly for Wright's liking. He watched the second hand crawl around the clock a few times, and then two cops walked in. One of them was a man he didn't recognize. The other was his partner, Belle Evans.

"Damn," Belle said. "You look lousy, Detective."

"I'm fine. It looks worse than it is." Actually, he felt like he'd been hit by a truck, but he didn't want to be taken off duty. Not with Peachey on the loose.

"He was here," he said. "I spotted him, but the air-cop shot me before I could grab him."

Belle's eyes widened. "Don't suppose you saw which plane he got on?"

"No. But if you can get me the security feed, I can point him out."

"Then we can track him to the gate, and match it to a destination."

"Right. And there's something else," Wright said. "How good are those cameras in the X-ray machines?"

"State of the art, I'd imagine," Belle said. "Why?"

"Do you think they could pick a serial number off a SIM card?"

Belle turned to the other cop. "Ask someone," she told him. "And get the security footage – ten minutes on either side of the incident. Got that?"

He nodded, and disappeared.

Belle said, "You're *very* clever, Damien."

"Not clever enough," Wright replied. "If I was, I'd have him by now."

"We'll get him. Don't worry."

"Call a judge, get a warrant to track the SIM card. Otherwise I won't be able to find him once I get there."

"Get where?" Belle asked suspiciously.

Wright shrugged, and winced as a flare of pain went off in his shoulder. "Whichever city Peachey landed in."

"*What?* No way are you going in person. Do you want me to list all the reasons that's insane?"

"I can catch him, Belle," Wright said. "I know how he thinks."

"I'll take that as a yes. One, you're in no condition to get out of bed, let alone go chasing a hit man. Two, wherever he is, it's probably way outside our jurisdiction, meaning you couldn't do anything even if you caught him. Three..."

She paused.

"Can't think of a three?" Wright asked.

Belle pursed her lips. "No, but those are two very good reasons."

A woman in green scrubs walked in with a clipboard. "Hello, Detective, I'm Doctor Keidis," she said. "How are you feeling?"

Wright ignored her. "I can catch him," he told Belle. "My legs are fine. And if I don't have jurisdiction wherever he is, I'll drag him to somewhere I do."

Belle looked doubtful. "Damien, I think you should rest."

"I agree," the doctor said, stretching Wright's eyelids open and shining a penlight in them.

"We're wasting time," he growled. "Get me that warrant."

"You have five minutes," the Ghost said. "Get what you need."

"We need longer than that," Benjamin said.

The Ghost looked at his watch. "Four minutes, fifty-two seconds."

Ash touched Benjamin's shoulder. "Don't push it," she whispered.

They were in Buckland's jet. They'd told the Ghost that they couldn't break into the Googleplex without their equipment, which was true. But it wasn't the main reason

Ash had wanted to go. She'd hoped Hammond Buckland would be here, that he would know some secret weakness of the Ghost's, that he would be able to rescue them.

He was nowhere to be seen.

Ash looked at the laptop bag with the Benji inside it, thinking of the built-in tranquillizer gun. But she didn't expect to have a chance to use it – too much assembly required, and they were being watched too closely.

They had left the bank vault at gunpoint, the alarms curiously silent, the cameras somehow disabled. The Ghost stayed several steps behind them at all times, his footfalls almost silent. Half the time, Ash wasn't even sure he was there.

He directed them to a car under a dead street light, where he sprayed Benjamin with something out of an aerosol can. Then he unlocked the boot remotely and told them to climb in. They obeyed. He told them to shut the lid, and they did that too. Ash wondered if he'd forgotten about the release button that was installed inside nearly all modern car boots on the inside. The sound of duct tape being peeled off a roll and slapped on the seam, strip after strip, told her he hadn't.

The ride was long and bumpy. Her phone said *no signal*, the reception muffled by the metal. She couldn't tell where they were going, and she couldn't call Buckland for help. The air inside the boot was cold and stank of carpet cleaner, telling Ash that the car was either new or a rental, since it made sense for the Ghost to clean it after abducting them rather than before.

She pictured him vacuuming, scrubbing, removing every trace they had ever existed – and she wondered where they would be by then.

He had been so careful. Now, in the plane, Ash doubted she'd have the opportunity to shoot him with the Benji. But she wasn't going to waste it if it came.

She picked up the bag and put it by the door.

"Three minutes, forty-six seconds," the Ghost said.

Ash picked up a small cylinder with a button on the end.

"What's that?"

"The trigger," she said.

"Give it to me."

She handed it over. He slipped it into his pocket.

The thought of doing a job with someone other than Benjamin as her tech support was, for Ash, the scariest part of this whole disaster. She took some clothes out of the overhead locker and moved towards the bathroom.

The Ghost said, "Stay in sight."

"I'm going to change," Ash said.

"Do it here."

"No."

He stared at her for a long moment. Ash doubted he had any compunction about causing her embarrassment. But he probably didn't want to make her or Benjamin mad. Fearful, yes. Angry, no. Fear would make them obedient. Anger would make them unpredictable.

He pointed the gun at Benjamin's face. "Throw me the clothes," he told Ash.

She did. He caught them one-handed, squeezed them, crushed them into strange shapes, and threw them back.

"Okay," he said. "You have three minutes and ten seconds."

Ash went into the bathroom and shut the door. She whipped out her phone.

Please, she thought. Come on.

Two bars of reception. Enough.

She typed: *b and i captured by ghost. headed 2 google now. being watched closely, dont call. plz help.*

She hit *send*. Then she stripped off her clothes as quickly as she could, pulled on the fresh ones, and opened the bathroom door—

—to reveal the Ghost looming in the doorway.

"Give me the phone," he said.

"What phone?"

He punched her in the throat. She gagged, eyes bugging out as she staggered back into the cubicle.

"Give it to me," he said.

Wheezing, Ash took it out of her pocket and held it out. He took it and it vanished in his hand.

"What did you tell him?"

There was no point lying. He would probably check the *sent* folder. "That we've been captured, we're going to the Googleplex, and we need his help."

The Ghost smiled, showing the perfect teeth that had entranced Ash only a day ago. "Good," he said.

Good? Ash felt her stomach drop. She'd led Buckland into a trap!

"He won't come," she lied.

"Not for you," he said. "But he will for Alice. He'll want to beat me there."

Benjamin and Ash looked at one another. Benjamin looked as confused as Ash felt.

"Revenge for stealing his emerald?" Benjamin asked.

"Payback for payback? No. Simple greed. He doesn't know how to switch it off."

Payback for payback, Ash thought. "What was the emerald payback for?"

The Ghost walked over to the door. "You haven't figured that out yet?"

Unease scuttled through Ash's brain. "Figured what out?"

"You never wondered who had the hit list before you? You thought you were Buckland's first teenage puppets?"

No way, Ash thought.

Benjamin's eyes were wide. "You worked for Buckland?"

"Until he stabbed me in the back," the Ghost said. "I've been waiting a long time to give him what he deserves. Why do you think I came to your school?"

The earth's rotation seemed to have tripled in speed. Ash thought of her conversation with Benjamin back home. *It's not like he tells us everything. We should be careful. We can't just assume Buckland is infallible.*

She thought of the way the Ghost had sprayed Benjamin with something, but not her.

"You planted something on me," she said. "That night. That's why you came to the dance. That's how you knew we were coming to California."

"Time's up," the Ghost said. "Let's go."

The Googleplex was silent. Still. Dark. It would be aphotic, Ash thought, if it weren't for that one halogen lamp.

The replica *T. rex* skeleton loomed out of the shadows, less comical at night. Teeth as big as waffle cones protruded from its jaw, ready to tear the flesh off the nearest Leptoceratops.

Ash lay on the grass, shivering. She couldn't go any closer to the buildings – three more steps and she'd be within range of the cameras.

She looked at her watch. Two minutes to go. I hope Benjamin's okay, she thought.

It had been physically painful to leave him with the Ghost. For all she knew, the Ghost had only pretended to be interested in Alice so he could get rid of Ash and take Benjamin to the buyer.

But if she'd refused to go, he would have killed her. She was certain of it.

Enough worrying. She plugged her headphones into the phone the Ghost had given her and dialled her own number.

The Ghost answered. "Yes?"

"I'm in position," Ash said. "Are you ready?"

"Yes."

"Let me talk to Benjamin."

There was a pause. *Ask yourself this. How far can you push me?*

Just a little further, she hoped.

"Ash?" It was Benjamin.

"Can he hear us?"

"No, just me."

"Good. Are you okay?"

"I'm all right. Are you?"

"Yeah," Ash said. "But I wanted to ask you something. How would you feel about retiring, after tonight?"

"You serious?"

"Very."

There was a pause. "It's been fun," he said. "But there must be safer ways to have a good time."

"That's what I've been thinking."

"You wouldn't miss it?"

"I think I would," Ash said. "And I still have a lot to make up for. But it's not worth dying over."

"No."

"And when we get home, I'm taking you out to dinner."

"Like..."

"Like a date," she finished. "If you still want to."

"You're just on the rebound," Benjamin said, "because the last guy turned out to be a jerk."

Ash wondered if the Ghost realized Benjamin was referring to him. "That was a shock," she admitted. "But I just want to do something normal. Be bored. Hang out, like when we were kids."

"You're saying it would be boring?"

"Your social plans are fascinating," the Ghost interrupted. His voice was low, distant. "But I don't have all night."

Ash frowned. "You said he couldn't hear us."

"He can't! I...how did you *do* that?"

The Ghost said, "If this takes much longer, I might change my mind about letting you live."

Ash rose into a sprinter's crouch. "Then hit the trigger already."

Thud. The halogen light clicked off. The phone died. All the active electronic devices in Mountain View went down in a fizz of malfunctioning circuitry. And every Google® search in the western United States came back with a 404 error.

The EMP generator Ash planted in the toilet cistern had done its job. There was no time to waste. She ran.

Her feet pounded across the grass, hard and fast. With all the lights out, she was sprinting through absolute blackness. It was hard to suppress the fear that she might be running towards a wall, even though she'd been staring at this empty courtyard for the last half-hour.

She had twenty seconds before the power came back on. As she ran, she pulled a weighted glow stick out of her pocket, bent it to start the chemical reaction, and threw it like a tiny javelin.

It tumbled to the ground up ahead, falling five or six metres short of the corner of Building 42, which loomed out of the darkness like the bow of an approaching ship.

Thirteen seconds. Ash held up the Benji, pressed the stock against her shoulder, pointed the muzzle slightly above the roof of Building 42, and pulled the trigger.

Wham! The recoil spun her around, nearly knocking her off her feet. The grappling hook sailed through the air, trailing the cable behind it, and clanked against the roof. Ash pulled the second trigger, and heard the *splink* as curved spikes popped out the sides of the hook. The motor in the Benji whirred as it reeled the cable back in.

Eight seconds until the lights and camera were back on. Ash held on tight, but there was still slack in the cable. Come on, she thought. Come on!

The grappling hook caught the edge of the roof, and Ash lurched forwards as the cable went taut, dragging her towards the wall. Her toes scraped along the grass as she fought to get her feet flat. Soon she was sliding on her heels like a water skier. When she was close enough, she jumped.

The wall rushed up to meet her and she hit it feet first. The cable was still retracting, and she had to run to keep from falling over. She sprinted up the wall in swift leaps, and then suddenly she was over the top.

She almost fell – the hook slammed back into the muzzle of the launcher, knocking her backwards, but she regained her balance on the edge of the roof. She stepped away from the drop as quickly as she could.

Her phone vibrated in her pocket as it rebooted. The halogen light clicked back on down below. The toilet water had short-circuited the EMP, right on time. She peered over the edge, and saw that the cameras had started moving again, but that her glow stick was all but invisible in the glare.

She had made it. She was in.

Benjamin and the Ghost would be in the sewer tunnels beneath the campus by now. She had to get down to the basement and let them inside.

There was a doorway on the other side of the roof, hopefully leading to a stairwell just like the one in Building 41. She ran over and tried the door. Locked. She pressed her palm against it, feeling for warmth – if there was an active alarm system, the circuitry would produce heat.

There was a warm patch, just under the handle. She shone the Benji's inbuilt torch into the seam, and saw the sensor – a thin square of metal, connected to the door frame by a red wire.

Ash selected laser mode, removed the tinted shield, and pulled the trigger.

A bright blue dot appeared on the door, quivering. Ash could already smell burning paint. She took aim at the wire, and watched the plastic coating bubble in the heat. Soon the copper was exposed. It glowed red for a moment, hissing, and then it cracked.

Ash switched off the laser and replaced the shield. The alarm should be disabled, theoretically.

She levelled the Benji at the upper hinge, selected grappling hook mode, and pulled the trigger.

The hook hit the door with a metallic thud, and the broken

hinge jingled to the ground. Ash repeated the action on the lower hinge, then grabbed the door and pulled. She stepped aside as it fell open, revealing a black hole.

Stairs materialized in the gloom as she clicked the torch back on. Her steps were agonizingly loud in the silence as she crept down on the balls of her feet.

There's nobody here, she told herself. The only security guards are in an office outside the gate.

The stairs ended at a corridor lined with offices. The glow of the torch bounced unsettlingly off the glass walls.

Basement, Ash thought. Got to find the basement.

She caught sight of another flight of stairs up ahead. She slipped towards them, descended, and found herself on the ground floor.

There was a sign pointing to the bathrooms. She followed it, figuring that the basement would have the plumbing in it, and would therefore be under the bathrooms, or pretty close.

Crack.

Ash's eyes widened. What was that?

She crouched, switching off the torch, and stayed as still as she could. She listened, but all she could hear was her heartbeat.

The sound had probably been some metal component of the building, swollen in the sun, shrinking as it cooled. Nothing to worry—

Footsteps.

She wasn't alone.

Ash stayed frozen. Until she could work out which direction the person was coming from, it wasn't safe to move. She could walk right into their line of sight.

Voices. There was more than one person.

So why are they here? Ash wondered. Are they Google® security, hunting me? Or are they other rescuers, searching for Alice?

Whatever they're paying you for this, Alice must be worth more. Way more.

Anyone searching for Alice wasn't necessarily a rescuer, she realized.

She saw a shadow moving, back the way she had come. That gave her the opportunity to run, but would she make it around the corner in time? And would they hear her?

Ash bit her lip. Move, or stay?

Too late. She could see their silhouettes now. They were facing her – if she moved, they would see.

"Do we abort?" one of them was saying.

"No," another said. "There'll be a tech team on their way to check out the fault. That EMP probably wasn't accidental, and when they figure that out, Google® will tighten security. We might not have another chance to acquire the package."

Her voice was familiar, rough, clipped, but Ash couldn't

place it. Whoever she was, she was getting closer, but at an angle. Perhaps she would walk right past Ash. Or maybe she would trip over her.

"If it wasn't an accident," the first guy said, "there's a good chance someone's in here with us, Sarge."

He was walking alongside the woman, further away than Ash. She thought she recognized his voice too. It was hard to be sure with the lights out, but it sounded like the eyebrowless man from the mine.

"All the more reason to get to the package as quick as possible," the sergeant said. "Otherwise he might escape with it."

" 'He'?"

The sergeant said nothing.

The package, Ash thought. That's how they think of Alice. She wondered if she could risk a low, gradual, soft step away from the two ex-soldiers. They might hear it. But if she didn't move, they might see her when they got too close.

"You think it's the Ghost," the man said.

"It could be anyone," she said.

"But you think it's him."

The sergeant turned to face him. "If I thought it was him," she hissed, "would I be standing here? After what he did to our team?"

The browless man said, "Yes."

"I'm not that brave. Now shut up. Whoever's here, they could be listening."

Ash held her breath as they got closer, closer – and then they were walking past, and rounding a corner out of sight.

She rose to her feet, slowly. Listened to their footsteps retreating. And then she kept moving towards the bathrooms.

That guy they're scared of, she thought. I'm about to let him in.

Did she feel bad about that? The Ghost was a monster – he'd killed dozens, maybe hundreds of people. But the sergeant and her comrade were equally horrible. There were fifty or sixty dead miners to attest to that.

If she let the Ghost in, he might murder them. Did she have the right to decide if they deserved to die?

This speculation was futile. If she *didn't* let him in, not only would Alice be at the mercy of the soldiers, but the Ghost would kill Benjamin for sure.

There was a door marked *Staff Only* near the bathrooms. Ash tried the handle. Unlocked. The door swung open to reveal another flight of stairs, down to the basement.

She switched her torch on again and started creeping down.

She'd come to the right place. Rows of pipes, squat and grimy, glistened in the torchlight. The concrete crunched under Ash's shoes as she searched for the manhole.

It was in the corner – a thick iron lid, locked closed by a wheel on the top. The wheel had one heavy spoke which protruded from the side and disappeared into a slot in the wall, ensuring that the manhole couldn't be opened from the other side.

Ash turned the wheel, pointing the spoke away from the wall, and lifted. The lid came up with surprising ease on recently oiled hinges.

She bent over the black pit beneath.

"Benjamin?" she whispered.

Nothing. Just the soft gurgling of distant waters.

"Benjamin?"

There was some kind of movement below. A clank, like a foot on a ladder.

Someone was coming up.

Ash backed away, raising the Benji. More soldiers? she thought. Or someone else? How many people are after Alice?

A face appeared above the lip of the hole. It was Benjamin.

"Damn it," Ash hissed. "You scared the hell out of me."

Benjamin didn't reply. His head hovered, skin drained of colour, staring at Ash. She had the sudden fear that it was mounted on a stick, that the Ghost had killed him and was taunting her—

Then the illusion broke as Benjamin climbed out, shaky,

but alive. He moved quickly away from the hole to stand beside Ash.

"You okay?" Ash said.

Benjamin shook his head as the Ghost emerged, eyes narrow, a finger over his lips.

No talking? Ash thought. Fine. I'm sick of listening to you.

The Ghost drew some kind of weapon that had been strapped to his back. At first, Ash thought it was a grappling-hook launcher like her own, but then she saw the barbed tip, daubed black to absorb light. It was a harpoon gun.

One of his nastier habits is shooting people with a flash-bang, impaling them with a harpoon, and dragging them out of sight.

Will Benjamin or I be on the end of that before the night's over? Ash wondered.

The Ghost pointed to the stairs. He wanted them to go up first.

Ash didn't like turning her back on him, but she didn't have much choice. Now that the Ghost was inside, he wouldn't kill Benjamin, at least not until he'd hacked the electronic locks, but Ash had no such protection.

With a last nervous glance at the harpoon, she climbed up the stairs, and heard Benjamin follow her. There was no other sound. When she reached the doorway at the top, she glanced back down to check why the Ghost wasn't following them – and was startled to see that he was. His footsteps and breaths were completely silent, as though he wasn't really there.

They walked in single file through the shadows of Building 42. Ash stopped at every intersection, waiting for the Ghost to signal left or right. She wasn't sure how he knew the way, but he always did. He jerked the harpoon gun one way or the other, and they kept moving.

Soon they came to a locked door. There was a keypad beside it.

The Ghost pointed to Benjamin, then to the door. Benjamin approached, his bottom lip between his teeth. His hand hovered over the keypad.

Ash could tell what he was thinking. If he got the door open, there was a strong chance the Ghost would kill them both. But if he didn't, the Ghost would torture them, and then, if that didn't work, kill them anyway and find his own way in.

The Ghost stepped forward and prodded Benjamin's back with the harpoon. Benjamin took a deep breath, and touched the *open* key.

Eight digits flashed up on the screen: *40707975*. That meant that every code would be four digits long and a factor of that number.

A computer would have had to work out a usable code by

trial and error. It would have divided 40707975 by the lowest possible four-digit combination, 1000, to see if the answer was a whole number. Then it would have tried 1001. Then 1002. It would have kept going until it found an answer that worked, by which time the five-second alarm in the door would have gone off.

Not Benjamin. The numbers were only on the screen for a moment, but Benjamin was already typing by the time they vanished. He hit four, then three, then eight and nine. The digits appeared on the screen as ****. He hit *OK*.

There was a pause.

The door lock clicked. He'd done it.

The Ghost whirled around, raising the harpoon gun one-handed, taking aim at Ash as he shoved Benjamin's back with his other arm, pushing him against the wall. He was going to kill them.

But Ash had seen this coming. She'd already taken aim and was reaching for the trigger of the Benji.

The point of the harpoon was rising rapidly. The line of fire swept up her torso and past her neck until the gun was levelled at her face. She leaned back like a limbo dancer, trying to duck out of the way without losing her aim.

He pulled the trigger. So did she.

She was quicker.

The Ghost yelped as an anaesthetic dart punctured his

thigh. The harpoon exploded out of his gun, rocketing past Ash and shattering the glass wall of a nearby office.

He dropped the gun and stumbled forward, his legs already buckling under him. Ash tried to step out of reach, but even drugged, he was too quick. His hand shot forward and closed around her throat. Muscles inflated under his sleeve, all along his arm and across his chest.

Ash let go of the Benji and grabbed the Ghost's fingers, trying to prise them from her neck. She couldn't breathe – he was crushing her windpipe, blocking her arteries. Her eyeballs felt like they were swelling in their sockets.

Benjamin had recovered and was pulling at the Ghost's arm. He grabbed the wrist and squeezed, squashing the tendons, trying to loosen his grip.

Ash felt the chokehold slacken a little, then a lot, maybe thanks to their combined strength, maybe thanks to the drugs. She ripped his hand away and gasped.

The Ghost fell to his knees and thumped face first to the floor.

"Whoa," Benjamin said.

"Yeah."

"You're fast."

"You're the one factoring eight-digit numbers in microseconds."

They stared down at the unconscious boy.

"How long will he be out?" Ash asked.

"Six hours, give or take."

"You said the tranquilliser was practically instant. How did he stay standing that long?"

"Beats me."

A puddle of drool was spreading out from under the Ghost's chin.

Benjamin said, "Shoot him again."

Ash hesitated. "What if he overdoses?"

Benjamin didn't reply.

"We can't *kill* him," Ash said.

"He was going to kill us."

"That doesn't make it okay."

"He's killed lots of other people."

"Nor does that."

Benjamin gritted his teeth. "He's a monster."

"He was, a minute ago. But now he's a sleeping kid. We can't murder a sleeping kid."

"So we just let him go?" Benjamin demanded. "When he wakes up, he'll come after us. Even if he doesn't, he'll hurt someone else."

"We'll shoot him again on our way out," Ash said. "Once his system has had some time to absorb the tranquillizer. Then we'll call the cops on him. He'll still be unconscious when they arrive. Okay?"

"They might not come," Benjamin said. "Or he could talk his way out of it when they do."

"We'll make sure that doesn't happen. He's getting locked up for a long time. Okay?"

After a moment, Benjamin nodded. "It doesn't feel right just leaving him here," he said. "But I trust you."

"Thanks" would have sounded too casual, so Ash didn't reply.

Benjamin turned to the door. "Ready to be heroes?" he asked.

"I just hope we're not too late," Ash said.

Benjamin opened the door and Ash followed him into the server room.

Peachey disassembled his gun for the fourth time, checked each component, and reassembled it. It was a nice piece – eighteen-round magazine, closed bolt, and a decent-length barrel, not one of those snub-nosed things that couldn't hit a cow in a pen.

Only minutes ago he'd seen the lights go out at the Googleplex. The car radio had gone dead at the same time, and when he'd checked his phone, the screen had been dark. EMP, he thought. Probably for my benefit, to get me in. But I'm supposed to wait for instructions. So I'll wait.

He was uneasy, though. Why would they tell him to wait for orders and then cut off his only means of communication?

Because they didn't expect me to be here yet, he realized. They told me to go to Mountain View and await instructions, but I came specifically to the Googleplex on my own initiative. Damn it.

So, now what? Should he sit in the car with a potentially broken phone all night, then buy a new one tomorrow morning and switch the SIM cards? That would probably be his best option – except that he wanted to go to the HBS International Bank on Castro Street. He wanted to find Ashley Arthur. And every second he spent at the Googleplex made it less likely she'd still be there.

It had been five minutes since he last attempted to switch on his phone. He took it out and tried again. "Come on," he muttered, pressing his thumb hard on the power switch, as though the amount of pressure would make a difference.

Maybe it did – the phone hummed and came to life.

Peachey waited as the company logo flashed up on the screen, the menu opened, and the phone searched for a signal. It found one, but didn't register any missed calls or messages.

Peachey frowned. Could the EMP have been coincidental? Surely not.

Beep. The phone registered a text message. Peachey opened it.

Michael, the main entrance to Building 42 is now unlocked. Follow the signs to the server room. Kill everyone inside, then anyone else you find in the building as you leave. Don't touch any of the equipment. $400,000 has been moved to an account accessible with the documentation you have been given. The same amount will be transferred after you leave. This will conclude your service.

There was a name at the bottom of the message. Female, old-fashioned, just as he'd suspected: *Alice B*. Peachey congratulated himself on his deductive reasoning, and opened the car door.

"Time to go to work," he said.

The Devil's Lair

Ash and Benjamin stared at the rows of server towers, square and dirty, illuminated only by the glow of various monitors and status lights. Cords overflowed from the tops of the towers like Medusa's hair. Dozens of cooling fans hummed in the darkness.

This was it – the brain of the world's biggest intelligence agency.

"What now?" Benjamin asked.

"We can't just call out," Ash said. "There could be someone guarding her."

Benjamin looked around doubtfully. "I don't think there's anyone in here," he said.

It *did* look like an ordinary server farm. But we've come this far, Ash thought. We have to look.

"You go that way, I'll go this way," she said. "I'll phone you if I find anything. It's on silent, right?"

"Yeah. Yours too?"

She nodded. "See you soon."

Benjamin tiptoed away down an aisle. Ash crept in the opposite direction.

This doesn't add up, she thought, looking at the towers of drives and processors. The security out there was tight, which would make this a perfect place to hold a prisoner – except that there's no security *inside*. The locks on the doors are one-way. It would be impossible to keep someone trapped in here without Google® knowing about it – they could just walk right out.

Ash had a sudden vision of a woman with her legs chopped off, screaming, bleeding, unable to drag herself to the door.

She shivered. Ridiculous. It would be far more practical to handcuff a prisoner to a wall-bracket or something...

She paused. Took a few steps backwards. Stared at the LCD monitor she'd just passed.

The screen was dark except for two words.

Hello, Hammond.

Ash blinked, trying to make sense of it. Was this something someone had Googled? Surely not – hundreds of searches were passing through this data centre every second. Why would this one be singled out?

There was a keyboard nearby. Ash tapped a random key to see if it was connected to the same processor.

It was, but the letter *K* appeared below the message, not alongside it. She hit delete a few times. The *K* disappeared, but she found that she couldn't erase the greeting. No one had typed it in.

Feeling silly, she typed, *Hello.*

The response was instant. *I wasn't sure you would come.*

Ash thought of how the Ghost had laughed when she'd told him Alice's name. She thought of the soldiers, here to pick up "a package".

She grabbed her phone and dialled Benjamin.

"Have you found Alice?" he asked.

"Um...I don't know."

One-handed, she typed, *Who are you?*

I am ALICE B. Nice to meet you, Hammond.

"You'd better come take a look at this," Ash said.

Benjamin appeared beside her a few seconds later, panting. "What do you mean, you don't know?"

Ash gestured at the screen. Benjamin frowned.

"She's not here," Ash said. "She's been moved."

"To a place with internet access? Generous kidnappers." Benjamin's eyes traced the screen, keyboard, and the nearest server stack. He nudged Ash.

"Hey," he said, pointing.

There was a grey box sitting on the shelf, plugged into the server, the screen and the keyboard.

"Does that look like a four-terabyte hard drive to you?" Benjamin asked.

"I don't get it," Ash said.

"Alice *has* been moved," Benjamin said. "From our local city library to here."

He stepped in front of the keyboard and typed, *What does ALICE stand for?*

Alice replied, *Artificial Linguistic Intelligence Computer Entity.*

"See?" Benjamin said. "That hard drive *is* her. She's the program that Kathy Connors wrote."

"But I've heard of Alice," Ash said. "My dad mentioned it. It was written back in the nineties. It's just a chatterbot, with a series of set responses to common questions. It imitates conversation, but it can't think. How could it send out a distress call? How could it even send a fax?"

"It can probably send emails, text messages – anything that's digital. This isn't just Alice, remember? This is Alice B.

Four terabytes is way more data than the original Alice software had, so this must be something new. And it's a lot more code than one programmer could write – so she must have taught it to write itself."

"But software can't *do* that," Ash said.

"Sure it can. Someone made another chatterbot awhile back that could learn – every time it received a question it didn't have an answer for, it asked someone else online and added their response to its database. Pretty soon it was talking like a real person. Suppose Connors did something like that? What if she went one step further and taught it to read? With internet access, it could learn pretty much everything there is to know."

Alice said, *Are you still there, Hammond?*

Benjamin said, "Ash, what if she taught it to talk to itself? That's all thinking is, really. What if this is the first example of true artificial intelligence?"

"Why does it believe we're Buckland?" Ash asked. "How does it know we know him?"

"Maybe..." Benjamin paused. "Alice is plugged into the system here, right? Maybe it faxed the note to the city library vault, digitally, and then waited for the coordinates to show up in the Google® search logs. Buckland's the one who did the search, so when she traced the IP address, it led back to him."

Hammond? Where are you?

Ash reached for the keyboard. *I'm not Hammond,* she typed. *I'm Ash.*

Hello, Ash. I am Alice.

"It doesn't seem that intelligent to me," Ash said. "Are you sure that—"

She broke off. The screen was filling up with text. It read:

Ashley Arthur birthday 21 October age 16 address 146 East Park Way blood type B negative school Narahm School for Girls associates Hammond Buckland Benjamin Whitely Kenneth Preen...

It went on and on. It listed Ash's parents, her classmates, all her teachers. It listed everyone Ash could remember meeting, and many people she couldn't.

"Whoa," she said. "How...what..."

"It knows everything Google® knows," Benjamin said. "It's probably the smartest thing on earth."

"But I didn't even tell it my last name!"

"It knows about Buckland, and it knows you're connected to him. It must have just taken a guess."

Ash sat down on the floor. There were no chairs and this was too much to take standing up.

"So what do we do?" she asked.

"I don't know. Take it back to the Connors family for the reward, I guess. That was the original plan."

There was a pause.

"There's one thing I don't get," Ash said. "It must be programmed to seek out information, or else it wouldn't learn anything. And the more it has access to, the smarter it becomes. Right?"

"Right."

"So why would it want to leave?" Ash asked. "There's more information here than anywhere else in the world. It said 'help me'. Why does it need our help?"

Benjamin squinted at the screen. "I don't know."

Ash felt unease growing in her belly. "How did Connors die again?"

"Her house was burned down," Benjamin said.

"By people who heard a rumour she'd murdered a child, right?"

"Yeah, that's...wait. You think Alice was behind that?"

"Like you said, it can send emails and texts. It can probably even do online banking. What if it knew she was going to sell it? Or switch it off?"

"So it had her *killed*?"

"And paid someone to steal it and take it to the city library. Another reservoir of knowledge for it to feed off."

"If it moved up from the library to here, where's it going next? Where does it want us to take it?"

A chill ran up Ash's spine. "Maybe it doesn't want to go

anywhere. Maybe the SOS was a trick. It wanted anybody who came to the library looking for it to be led into a trap."

"That doesn't make any sense," Benjamin said. "It may be the first self-aware computer, but in another sense it's just a talking box. What kind of trap could it possibly set?"

Alice said, *Hello, Peachey.*

Ash scrambled to her feet. "What the hell?"

Benjamin was pale. "It must know about him. It's trying to freak you out, that's all."

Ash typed, *I'm not Peachey. I'm Ash.*

"Peachey's in jail, right?" Benjamin said. "He won't get parole for decades, right?"

Alice said, *Hello, Peachey. Hello, Peachey. Hello, Peachey.*

And the server farm door clicked closed somewhere behind them.

He's here, Ash thought. Oh god, he's here. We're dead.

She'd had nightmares about Michael Peachey. She would be running through the corridors of HBS, heart in her mouth, legs growing heavy and clumsy, and she could hear him getting closer, hear his voice – *You can't get away from me! No one ever does!* – and then she'd fall, grazing her hands, and when she turned she'd see his face, not stony like the mugshot on TV, but lit up with fury and madness.

Ash gripped the Benji. There were eleven tranquillizer darts left in the magazine. But she doubted she would be as successful as she had been with the Ghost. He had needed her. She'd had time to find an opportunity to shoot him.

Michael Peachey would kill her and Benjamin on sight. No questions, no negotiation, no "Unlock this door for me and I'll let you live." Just six bullets in their brains, lungs and hearts.

"What do we do?" Benjamin hissed, eyes wide.

Think, Ash. Think!

"The door," she whispered. "He's going to have to move away from it to search the room. We'll get out while his back is turned."

"He'll hear us open it."

"So we'll shut it behind us and run like hell." She unplugged the hard drive and slipped it into her bag. Alice's words vanished from the screen. "You ready?"

Benjamin nodded. "Let's do it."

For the first time, Ash was struck by how brave he was. A coward would have refused to move, hoping Peachey would go away or that he could be talked down. But while Benjamin was often frightened, he never let the fear make decisions for him. Cowards hope, heroes act.

They crept along a row of servers, listening for Peachey's footsteps. Ash heard nothing but her own breaths, which felt terrifyingly loud. If Peachey wasn't moving, he was probably listening for them. She willed her shoes not to squeak.

They reached the end of the aisle. Ash poked the tip of the Benji around the corner, looking for a reflection of the door in the tip of the grappling hook.

Peachey was there.

Ash withdrew the Benji, slowly, so Peachey wouldn't see the movement. He had been standing with his back to the door, gun drawn.

She leaned close to Benjamin. "No good," she breathed. "He's right against the door, and it doesn't look like he's going anywhere."

Benjamin swallowed. "He knows we're here. And he knows there's no other way out."

Ash stared at the floor. Thought hard.

"Stalemate," Benjamin said. "We can't move until he does, and he won't until we're dead."

"He might not realize we know he's here."

"So?"

"So we can trick him." But, Ash thought, we need bait.

Benjamin had known her long enough to tell what she was thinking. "No way, Ash," he said. "We stick together."

"If we stick together, we'll die in here." She handed him the Benji. "Wait until you get a clear shot."

"Then let me be the bait," he whispered. "You've got better aim than me anyway."

"You can't run as fast as I can," Ash said. "This is the best way."

"I'm not letting you leave me here while you walk into the firing line!"

She hesitated. She didn't like it any more than he did. But she knew it was their only chance.

"Don't be a hero," she said. "Shoot him in the back."

She didn't give him any more time to argue with her, or give herself the chance to change her mind. She slinked away, moving towards the opposite side of the server room.

She still hadn't heard Peachey move. She tried to take it as a good sign – if he'd known they had spotted him, he would have been sneaking away so they couldn't trap him.

On the other hand, maybe he was just treading very lightly.

Ash reached the far side of the room. Took a deep breath. It went against every instinct to make a loud noise while she knew Peachey was listening, but the plan depended on it.

She pressed one foot against a server tower and kicked it over. At least, she tried to – but it didn't move.

She looked down, and saw that it was welded to the floor. Of course, she thought. This is California. If the towers were loose, earthquakes would knock them over every other day. Damn it.

She didn't have anything to break the metal seal, so she unplugged one of the servers from the tower, and pulled. It fell to the floor with a mighty crash.

"Crap!" she yelled. Then, quieter, but still loud enough for Peachey to hear, she said, "Pick that up, will you?"

She was rewarded with a soft footstep. Peachey had heard and he was coming her way.

She kept making noise, stamping her feet and rattling computers. If she went silent now, he would suspect a trap. He might turn around and see Benjamin sneaking up on him.

She kept her eyes on the tower closest to the door, waiting for him to appear beside it. She crouched slightly, legs like coiled springs, ready to run the moment she saw him.

"What about these cables?" she said aloud. "Should we take them too?"

Another footstep. He was coming.

Don't look back, Peachey, she thought. Eyes straight ahead.

It took all her restraint not to start running now, to get as far away from him as possible, and hide. But Benjamin was depending on her.

Peachey stepped into view, gun barrel raised.

Ash exploded into motion, dashing away between two server towers. She heard a *crack*, and a monitor burst near her head as a bullet plunged into the screen. She kept her head down. Kept running.

She could hear him behind her, shoes slapping against the tiles, hard, heavy breaths. She reached the wall, hit it palms first, ran sideways. *Blam!* A ragged hole flowered where her hands had been.

Any time, Benjamin! she thought. I can't take much more of—

Her foot caught on a trailing power cable and slipped out from under her. She cried out as she fell, her fear of Peachey momentarily overwhelmed by the fear of breaking her neck, and she covered her face with her arms.

Her knee hit the floor first – it felt like a firecracker had gone off in the joint. She tumbled sideways, banging a hip. He's right behind me, she thought. Got to run.

Too late. As she scrambled to her feet, Peachey was already there, his pistol pointed at her head, his finger on the trigger. There was nothing she could do.

He saw her face. Stared.

"You?" he said in disbelief.

Then he dropped the gun.

Ash stared. Was he surrendering? Why would he do that?

Peachey looked down at his empty hand, apparently

perplexed. A dark stain appeared on his shirt, growing like a fast-spreading cancer. When he touched it, his fingers came back bloody.

He twitched as another hole opened up in his chest, and this time Ash heard the cough of a silenced low-calibre pistol. Her first thought was that Benjamin had found a gun and opted to use that instead of the Benji. But where? Why?

Peachey glared at Ash as though he knew this was somehow her fault. He took a step towards her, one hand clenching into a fist.

Cough. Another spray of blood from his torso, and he fell like a tree in a storm. Hit the floor face first, eyes rolling wildly, then fluttering closed.

Ash scrambled back behind a tower as the browless ex-soldier and his sergeant approached, weapons still drawn.

"Christ," the man said. "I thought he'd never go down."

"Is he dead?" the sergeant asked.

The man looked at the puddle of blood growing beneath Peachey's body. "Heart's still pumping," he said. "He'll bleed out soon."

"Good," she said. "Find the package. It should still be connected to the main server. That way."

Ash didn't see which way the woman had pointed, but they were getting closer. She backed away, edging around the tower to stay out of sight.

"If the TRA wanted the hard drive," the man was saying, "why did they have us plant it here in the first place?"

"Don't know, don't care," the sergeant replied. "I receive the instructions, I follow them, I get paid."

"I'm just saying, this is the third time we've had to steal it. Doesn't that seem weird to you?"

"Then it's the third time you get paid for the same package. You should be thankful. You should be especially thankful that this time you don't have to break into a burning house to do it."

Ash heard their footsteps getting closer. She pressed her back against the tower as though she could melt into it and become invisible.

They stole Alice from Connors' house, she realized. And they think their instructions are coming from the TRA. But if they shot Peachey, then where's Benjamin?

She hoped he'd seen them come in and had the good sense to run, but it didn't seem likely. He was too loyal – he'd never leave her in danger. So he must still be here, somewhere. And once the soldiers discovered the hard drive wasn't where it was supposed to be, and that Peachey didn't have it, they'd start searching the rest of the room. She and Benjamin would be in danger.

Ash heard them moving past the tower, back towards where she'd found Alice. Once she judged that they were out of earshot, she pulled out her phone and called Benjamin.

He answered immediately. "Ash, who are those guys?" he whispered.

"The ones from the mine. Where are you?"

"Near the door. You?"

"Next to Peachey's body. But I can't get to you – the soldiers are in the way."

"I've got the Benji. I can take them out."

"You can't. They're both armed and they're both pros."

"I have to try."

"No you don't." Ash bit her lip. "I want you to leave and slam the door behind you so they hear it. Then hide somewhere and let them run past. I'll slip out after them and go to the Amphitheatre Parkway outside. I'll wait for you there. Got it?"

There was silence.

"Got it?" she said again.

"Okay. I hope you know what you're doing."

"Almost always. See you soon."

She hung up, crouched, and waited.

She heard a clang from near the main server. The browless man cursed loudly. "It's not here," he said.

"I see that. Maybe the dead guy has it."

They were coming back. Now would be a really good time, Benjamin, Ash thought.

The door slammed closed as soon as she'd completed the thought. Not for the first time, Ash wondered if she and Benjamin were psychically linked.

"Damn it!" the woman hissed.

Ash heard her and her comrade sprint towards the door, just as she'd expected. They opened it, ran through, and kept running as it swung closed. She hoped Benjamin had had time to hide.

She waited a few seconds before moving. If one of them had thought to stay behind in case the thief doubled back, they would return quickly. But no one came.

Ash emerged from behind the server tower and walked towards the door. This long, hard mission was finally coming to—

Something grabbed her ankle.

She looked down and screamed as she saw Peachey leering up at her from the end of a long trail of bloody smears and handprints. He was holding the gun.

Ash tried to pull away, but his other hand was clenched too tightly around her ankle. For a man who was bleeding to death, he didn't seem to have lost much strength. She bent down over him, reaching for the gun, trying to snatch it from his grip.

He took aim at her face, and pulled the trigger.

Ash crumpled to the ground.

Showdown

The pain was incredible.

For a moment Ash wasn't sure what had happened. One of her ears was chiming, so loud she couldn't think. It was like someone was beating a gong right beside her head. She could tell she was on the floor, but not which way was up. Her balance was completely gone.

Her cheek felt as though someone had flung lava onto it. She slapped herself in the face, trying to put out the flames. Her skin was hard and cracked, cauterized by the muzzle flash. The bullet must have missed her by only—

She moaned in horror as her fingers reached her ear. The bullet had torn a narrow chunk out of it, exposing the cartilage in the tip. There was no blood – the heat had sealed the wound.

Turning her head, Ash saw Peachey lying next to her.

He was lining up a second shot.

Terror took over, and she lashed out, driving her fist into his face as hard as she could. She'd never hit anyone with her bare hand before. Her knuckles stung as they collided with his cheekbone.

She did it again. And again.

The gun went off. Ash felt another sizzling rush of hot air, but the bullet missed her.

She hit him a fourth time, a fifth, a sixth. His fingers were still wrapped tightly around the grip of the gun.

Seventh. Eighth. Each wet smack made her want to puke. Her hand was covered in blood.

He dropped the gun.

She grabbed it, threw it as hard as she could, and collapsed. She heard it skitter away across the floor. Only now did she realize she'd been screaming like she was on fire.

Peachey was deathly still, his eyes wide open and staring at the ceiling. Looking at his mashed-up face, Ash realized that he might be dead. She could be a murderer.

He made me do it, she thought. He would have killed me if I hadn't stopped him. And he was dying anyway.

The notion didn't make her feel any better.

She staggered to her feet. Her ear felt like someone was squeezing it with pliers. Got to get out of here, she thought. Got to get to the Parkway. Peachey's out of the game, but those two soldiers are still here.

The game. It didn't feel like a game any more. Prodding the wound, she thought, What the hell am I going to tell Dad?

She could pretend she'd been mugged. But then she'd have to lie, not just to him, but to the police. To doctors at the hospital. To teachers and friends when she got back to school. She was so sick of lying. Besides, if he thought she'd been mugged, her father might never let her leave the house again.

Ash found herself wondering if that would be such a bad thing. Her career as a thief was probably over, after all. She had relied on her ability to blend in. A disfigurement like this would make that much harder.

Do ears grow back? she wondered. Because if you don't wear your earrings for a while, the holes close up, right?

But she knew this wouldn't be the same.

A salty tear trickled over her burns; burns that might never heal, stinging her. She opened the server room door and stumbled out, leaving all the blood and bullet holes behind her.

She thought of her first meeting with the Ghost. *You're just, uh, really pretty.* Maybe she'd never hear those words again. Not even from a psychopath.

How is Benjamin going to take this? she wondered. Will he even be able to look at me?

She lurched towards the stairs that led down to the lobby, trying to hold down the vomit that threatened to rush up her throat every time she imagined what she must look like. What she would look like for the rest of her life.

She reached the stairs.

The Ghost was standing at the bottom of them.

Ash's heart punched her ribs, and as she turned to run, a harpoon swept past her head like a swooping bird. It slammed into the ceiling above her, and then the cable went taut. She heard a whizzing sound, getting closer and closer as the Ghost flew up the stairs.

She sprinted down the corridor, her wounds forgotten, a tsunami of adrenaline sweeping away the pain. She reached a T-junction and turned left. She heard the Ghost land somewhere behind her and give chase.

She turned right, her hand squeaking along a glass wall.

He has weapons, magic tricks and no conscience, she thought. But I bet I can run faster.

And then she saw another flight of stairs ahead – leading up.

Every flight she went up took her further away from the exit. But if she tried to double back, the Ghost would have gained a lot of ground, bringing her within range of his harpoon.

And every second she spent standing here thinking about it brought him closer.

She made her decision. She ran up the stairs, pushed open the door at the top – and realized she'd made a terrible mistake.

She was back on the roof. And this time there was no time to make a slide out of the solar panels.

"No!" she hissed. She ran over to the edge, and looked down. The trees below were tiny. She was way too high to jump.

She scanned the roof for hiding places. There was nowhere.

There must be a way to buy some time. She rummaged through her backpack, looking for something she could use. Duct tape, spare rounds for the Benji, glow sticks. All useless.

She started moving back towards the door, hoping to get behind it before—

The door burst open. The Ghost loomed in the frame like the Grim Reaper, harpoon gun by his side.

He raised it.

"Don't," Ash said.

"Why?" He sounded surprised. Perhaps he was used to his victims begging, rather than issuing orders.

Ash talked quickly. Words were her only remaining defence. "Because you don't have to," she said. "I'm unarmed. I'm no threat. And your problem is with Buckland, not with me. Killing me won't get you to him."

"No," he said. His expression was unreadable. "But what's in your bag might. The hard drive is on his list. It was always my goal – why do you think I put your friend's name up on my website?"

"*You* did that?" Ash gaped at him. "But...how did you know we would hide in the bank?"

"Buckland is very predictable," the Ghost said.

He was done talking. His finger tightened on the trigger.

Click. For a moment Ash thought the harpoon gun had jammed. Then she saw the browless man and his sergeant standing in the doorway behind the Ghost. The browless man had his pistol raised – the click had been the hammer pulling back.

The Ghost whirled around to face them. Took aim.

"Ghost," the sergeant breathed. Her revolver trembled in her hand.

The Ghost smiled faintly. "And you are?"

The browless man said, "Drop the gun."

"No."

Ash crept backwards. This was a disaster waiting to happen, and she didn't want to get caught in the crossfire.

"You can't win this," the browless man said. "Two guns against one. You shoot either of us, the other one will shoot you."

"If you know who I am," the Ghost said, "you know the bullets will pass right through me. I won't be harmed."

"I don't believe in any of that crap."

The Ghost's gun didn't waver. "You sure?"

The browless man fired, and the bullet pinged off the harpoon gun, even as the Ghost was squeezing the trigger.

The man fired again, but missed – he'd backed into the sergeant, throwing off his aim. The bullet sparked across the rooftop.

The Ghost fired.

The harpoon went straight into the browless man's chest, skewering him. The barb exploded out his back and plunged into the sergeant's open mouth.

They fell to the ground, joined together. Ash heard the sergeant's neck break as the fall twisted it.

The Ghost turned to face Ash. She'd made it to the edge of the rooftop, and was standing still, one hand in her backpack.

The Ghost reeled the harpoon back in. The two dead bodies flopped around wetly as the spear was dragged out of them.

He turned to face her, ready to fire again.

"I wouldn't do that," Ash said.

"No," he replied. "You probably wouldn't."

He raised the gun.

Ash held the hard drive out over the edge. The drive with Alice B on it.

She said, "Shoot me, and this will fall."

"You'll still be dead."

Ash shrugged. "And you'll have lost what you came here for."

She let a bit of the cord slip through her fingers. The drive jerked downwards. The Ghost lunged forwards, and she caught it again.

"Uh-uh," she said. "Stay back."

He was eight, maybe ten metres away. Too far to make a grab for the hard drive, but close enough that if he chose to shoot, he wouldn't miss.

"You can't stand there for ever," he said.

"Neither can you. In less than..." she checked her watch, "...one hour, the sun will come up. Google® security will do their regular morning check, and when they find the dead body in the server room, they'll call the cops. I'm thinking you'll want to be gone before they arrive."

"So will you."

"Maybe," Ash said. "But I'm only facing charges of breaking and entering. You're up for double homicide, at a minimum."

The Ghost said nothing.

"You're going to leave," Ash told him. "When I see you on the ground down below, I'm going to put the drive here. You can come back up and get it – I'll be gone by the time you arrive."

"How do I know you won't just take it with you?"

"I don't want it," Ash said. "I came here to rescue a human being. I was trying to do the right thing, for once. Turns out no one here needs saving, and I'm not interested in owning a murderous talking box."

The Ghost took a step forwards.

"I'll drop it," Ash warned.

"I don't think you will." He took another step.

Ash let the cord drop a little further. He kept coming.

"I think you realize that if you drop it, you'll have no more leverage," he said. "And there'll be nothing to stop me killing you."

He was six metres away now. "But if you hand it over," he said, "I'll let you go."

He was an excellent liar – for a second, Ash almost believed him. The awkward smile he'd flashed her at the dance was back.

"Why would I hurt you?" he said. "Once I have the hard drive, I can just leave."

He was four metres away.

"Hey," Ash said, "you can make people disappear, walk through walls and pull knives out of thin air, right?"

He frowned. "So?"

Ash smiled grimly. "So, can you fly?"

And she tossed the drive over the edge.

"No!" the Ghost roared. He reached out, tried to grab the drive, missed. It spun and tumbled through the void, vanishing into the darkness. There was a distant *crash* as it splintered into thousands of useless pieces.

The Ghost turned his murderous gaze on Ash, teeth bared, and pointed the harpoon gun at her heart.

She was backed up against the edge of the roof. There was nowhere to run.

"Can *you*?" he growled.

Ash didn't answer. Instead, she stepped backwards off the edge.

Down to Earth

Ash fell.

The Ghost was sucked out of sight and replaced by a blur of windows. Ash saw her reflection for the first time since getting shot – a blackened cheek shimmered back at her, in a halo of fluttering hair.

Her guts felt hollow. Her arms and legs flailed uselessly. She couldn't fly.

But she wasn't going to die, either. Not today.

She shoved a hand into her pocket and grabbed the canister of compressed hydrogen sewn into the lining.

Shouldn't have let me change on the plane, she thought. She hit the button.

The balloons in her clothes swelled up, starting with the ones near her pocket, and spreading out to cover the rest of her body. A hissing filled the air as the pressure equalized.

With growing panic, she saw that she was still accelerating. The balloons weren't slowing her down at all. She should have expected that, since all objects fall at the same rate regardless of their weight – Benjamin's invention was designed to decrease the force with which she'd hit the ground, not the speed.

That reasoning had been easy to accept in his basement laboratory. It was much harder now, plummeting towards the ground at two hundred kilometres per hour.

But she trusted Benjamin. She had always trusted Benjamin.

And so she did what he'd taught her, spreading her arms and legs like a skydiver, increasing the wind drag, fighting the urge to try and stay upright. If she landed on her feet, both legs would snap like plywood.

Her clothes bulged more and more. The balloons started squeezing her chest, making it hard to breathe. She shut her eyes as the ground rushed up towards her. At the last second, she crossed her swollen forearms over her face, protecting it from the impact.

WHAM! It was like getting kicked in the sternum. The shock rippled out across her limbs as her head bounced against her inflated sleeves. Suddenly she was in the air again – she'd bounced off the ground like a giant beach ball. She spun sideways in the air, landing on her back, and with a sharp bang, a balloon near her knee popped.

The hydrogen squealed out of her clothes swiftly, and she sank to the ground. She sat up dizzily as her body returned to its normal shape.

Looking down to see what had popped the balloon, she saw the shattered hard drive – all that was left of the first non-human intelligence on earth. She laughed.

"Well done, Alice," she said. "You got me."

"And now *I've* got you."

Ash choked on her breath. She tried to get up, look around, see who had spoken, but someone was already grabbing her from behind. She felt the familiar cold sting of handcuffs closing around her wrists as she was hauled to her feet.

No, she thought. No, no, no!

"Hello, Ashley," Detective Wright said. His nose looked broken, and he was favouring one arm, but there was an enormous smile on his face. "I'm arresting you as an accomplice to the murder of Hammond Buckland. You do not have to say anything, but it may harm your defence if you do not mention, when questioned, something which you later rely on in court. Anything you do say may be given in evidence."

Murder? "I didn't kill Hammond Buckland!" Ash protested. "You're making a mistake!"

Wright's radio crackled. "Detective?"

Wright held down the button. "Go ahead."

Is this the end? Ash wondered. Is it over? Am I caught?

Maybe that would be best. She was so tired. Tired of running, tired of fighting, tired of hiding. Maybe this was the only way out of that life.

But after all the things she'd done, was she really going to get locked away for the one thing she *didn't* do?

No, she decided. There was a way out of this and she was going to find it.

"Sir, we've found Michael Peachey," the radio was saying. "He's beat up pretty bad, but we've got the paramedics working on him, and they reckon he's going to pull through. He'll be back under lock and key in no time."

Wright smiled. "Some days," he told Ash, "I really love my job."

And then, hands still behind her back, Ash pulled a magnesium flare off Wright's belt and set it off.

A blade of fire lanced out from the end as the hydrogen in the air ignited, quadrupling the heat. Wright recoiled from the brightness, yelling. Every instinct told Ash to drop the blazing stick, but she held on, teeth clenched. She spun the flare in her hands like a baton, turning the fiery tip to face the chain that linked her cuffs together. Then she *pulled*.

The red-hot metal snapped, and she was free.

She didn't give Wright time to regain his sight. She sprinted into the darkness, away from him, away from Peachey, away from Alice, away from the Ghost, away from this whole nightmare. She tripped, rolling along the grass, stifling the flames on her jeans, and then she clambered to her feet and didn't stop running until suddenly she found herself kilometres away, legs giving out beneath her.

Epilogue

A week had passed.

After escaping from the Googleplex, Ash had found Benjamin waiting for her on the Parkway, just as they'd planned. They trudged back to HBS International, where they found Hammond Buckland, holding Benjamin's ransom in a briefcase, waiting for the bank to open so he could let them out. He was astonished to see them already loose, and asked hundreds of questions on the flight home. They told him everything, except what they had learned about his connection to the Ghost. Sometimes, Ash knew, it was safest to feign ignorance. She wasn't sure she trusted Buckland any more.

"You don't have to do this," Benjamin said.

"I know," Ash replied.

It was almost ten at night and they were walking, hand in hand, through the quiet streets of their home town. A woman snored on a nearby bus stop bench. A possum in an overturned rubbish bin froze as they passed, eyes gleaming in the dark, and waited until they were gone before continuing to rummage.

Her burns were mostly healed, but she still covered them with make-up, especially in front of her dad. She'd been keeping her hair draped over her chipped ear, and it was getting easier to remember not to casually tuck it back. At first, when she looked in the mirror, she had been reminded of a feral cat. Now, gradually, the damage was becoming a part of her.

She and Benjamin had just been on their first date. Dinner at a secluded restaurant, dessert at a rooftop café, and then a long walk through the paths and parks of the city. Ash had never seen him look so happy. Why did I wait so long? she wondered.

But now they were here and it was time for Benjamin to go home.

"Are you sure?" he said.

"I'm sure."

"There's no going back."

"I know."

"You don't have to do this," he said again.

"No," she said. "But I'm going to."

He nodded. His eyes were beginning to shine with tears.

"Come visit me sometime?" she said.

"I will," he said.

She kissed him on the cheek, and turned to walk away. When she looked back, he was still standing under the street lamp. Her heart felt like it would burst. But this was one place she wouldn't let him follow her.

"Go home," she said.

"I'll miss you."

"You too – but you've gotta go."

Benjamin bit his lip. "Goodbye, Ash," he said, and then he walked away, out of the light. She waited until he was out of sight, and then she turned back to the building they'd stopped at.

She'd tried giving away the money she'd stolen, she'd tried stealing things only from bad people, and she'd even tried her hand as a rescuer. Nothing had eased her conscience. There was only one thing left.

She walked into the police station.

Detective Damien Wright was in the foyer, sifting through an evidence bag. He saw her, and did a double take, eyes widening, hands already shrinking into fists. He lunged forwards – then stopped, confused. She wasn't running away.

"I'm here to turn myself in," Ash said. And she held out her hands for the cuffs.

Author's Note

All the characters of *Hit List* are fictional, along with most of the locations – the Hallett State Remand Centre, HBS International Bank, and Narahm School for Girls.

But there are, as always, some truths among the lies. There really is a program called ALICE that mimics human conversation. It was designed by Dr. Richard Wallace in the nineties, and has since become open-source – you can talk to a primitive version of it on jackheath.com.au.

The learning chatterbot that Benjamin referred to also exists. It's called Jabberwacky, and while I think a future adaptation of Jabberwacky is far more likely to become self-aware than ALICE is, I decided the name wouldn't sound as good on an SOS. Call it artistic licence.

Unless this book has somehow outlasted one of the world's most successful companies, you probably already know that Google® is also real. They are worth $39 billion, they know more than the CIA, and they let their employees take their dogs to work. If you look at Building 41 of the Googleplex on Google Earth, you'll see that it's covered in solar panels, and that there are endless pools not so far away.

Vincent van Gogh's ear has never been found.

Acknowledgements

Thank you to my amazing partner, Venetia, whose strength and love make everything possible.

Thanks to my family, Mum and Dad and Tom, whose pride is the most inspiring part of my life.

Thanks to Sam MacGregor, whose enthusiasm helped this book get off the ground.

Thank you to my terrific agent, Clare Forster; you are the reason I tell all aspiring writers to get agents.

Thank you to Claire Craig, who always knows when to rein me in and when to let me off the leash. Your passion for your work is invaluable. Thanks to the rest of the team at Pan, especially Sue Bobbermein, Brianne Collins, Ali Lavau, Kate Nash, and Cate Paterson. You guys have always got my back.

Thank you to the guards at the Belconnen Remand Centre for giving me the tour and answering my questions. Every prison scene I ever write will be better thanks to you.

Thank you to Google®, for making the rest of my research so easy.

Thanks to a few writers who shared their wisdom and gave me encouragement and who are overdue for a mention: Tristan Bancks, Michael Gerard Bauer, Amanda Betts, Gavin Bishop, Ben Brown, Melanie Drewery, Melaina Faranda, Andy Griffiths, Martin Harrison, Gregg Hurwitz, Ingrid Jonach, Ross Kinnaird, William Kostakis, Jeff Lindsay, Dawn McMillan, Linda McNabb, Kyle Mewburn, Patrick Ness, Michael Pryor, Helen Fields, Berndt Sellheim, KJ Taylor, and Mark Walden.

And lastly, thank you to the fans. It's a pleasure and a privilege to lead you on this journey.

About the Author

Jack Heath is an award-winning author of action-adventure books. He started writing his first book when he was thirteen years old and had a publishing contract for it at eighteen.

When he's not writing, Jack is performing street magic, composing film music, teaching or lecturing at schools and festivals, or playing a variety of instruments, including the piano and the bass guitar. He stoically ignores his lack of qualifications or training in any of these areas.

Jack lives in Canberra, Australia, with his fiancée, Venetia, and their cat, Onyx.

jackheath.com.au

Don't miss Ash and Benjamin's first heist...

What would you do for $200 million?

**Would you break into a billionaire businessman's
top-security skyscraper?**

Would you drive a priceless sports car off the roof?

**Would you fly a helicopter with only a handbook
to guide you?**

**And would you take on an unstoppable hitman
intent on your destruction?**

For teen thieves Ash and Benjamin, it's a no-brainer...

*"If you love full-on action films then you
will love this book."*
bookzone4boys.blogspot.com